I0636498

Stutter Creek
by
Ann Swann

5 Prince Publishing
Denver, Colorado

This is a fictional work. The names, characters, incidents, places, and locations are solely the concepts and products of the author's imagination or are used to create a fictitious story and should not be construed as real.

5 PRINCE PUBLISHING AND BOOKS, LLC
PO Box 16507
Denver, CO 80216
www.5PrinceBooks.com

ISBN 13:978-1-939217-49-3 ISBN 10:1-939217-49-0
Stutter Creek
Ann Swann
Copyright Ann Swann 2013
Published by 5 Prince Publishing

Front Cover Viola Estrella

First Edition/First Printing June 2013 Printed U.S.A.

5 PRINCE PUBLISHING AND BOOKS, LLC.

What people are saying about Ann Swann...

Like the song, this heart-tugging novel takes us on a journey revealing that love is indeed a many-splendored thing. More than pounding heartbeats. More than passionate kisses. It carries with it the weight of our responsibility in nurturing relationships. Whether we read this before or after our own mistakes, All for Love has a message we need to hear.
-Gwen P. Choate

ALL FOR LOVE is not your average romance novel. I would call it Literary Fiction and Family Drama at its best.
You don't just read a novel by Ann Swann - you literally experience it. I would recommend this novel to anyone who enjoys a story with depth and heart.
-Deanna S.

This book is dedicated to my family, my friends,
and to the lovely readers who keep asking
when the next book is coming.

Acknowledgements

I would like to acknowledge the many-hatted Bernadette Soehner for all she does to keep us inspired, as well as the talented cover artist, Viola Estrella.

Stutter Creek

Chapter One

Amanda Myers was making a conscious effort to keep her heavy foot off the Toyota's gas pedal when she spied, what appeared to be, a small boy standing beside the road. An old-fashioned newsboy cap nearly obscured his tiny face.

Mandy hit the brake and steered the Celica toward the gravel shoulder. Even though she would be late for her evening shift at The Water House Bar & Grill, there was no way she could simply drive past a small boy standing beside the road.

With a practiced hand, she quickly texted her coworker, Myra, and asked her to concoct a cover story for her tardiness. She had intended to call her mom back home in Sunset, New Mexico and let her know how easy her college midterms had been. But that would have to wait.

The kid had seemed very small in silhouette—maybe five or six years old—and no house or vehicle in sight.

When Myra texted back to say the boss was on the warpath, Mandy replied, "Well, just tell him I stopped to pick up a boy on the edge of town. That should really turn his face red!" It was an inside joke. Everyone knew when the boss's face was red it was wise to give him a wide berth.

Myra sent back a row of question marks.

"L8R," Mandy responded. She looked all around. She had assumed the little guy would come dashing up to the car as soon as she had come to a stop. But even when she could no longer hear the crunch of her tires on gravel, he still hadn't materialized.

I didn't pass him by that much.

Craning her neck to see past the Toyota's blind spot, Mandy dropped the phone into the center console drink holder and shoved the gearshift into park. A thick stand of live oaks cast a deep shadow over the bar ditch. The setting sun made the trees appear as black-paper cutouts in a landscape collage.

After checking her mirrors to make sure no one was behind her, Mandy pressed the button to lower the passenger-side window.

It was almost all the way down when a man yanked open the door and exploded into her world like a tornado into a trailer park. Her hand flew to the gearshift, but she couldn't engage it. Even as her flight instinct kicked in, part of her mind was telling her this was almost certainly the same strange guy who had requested her section at the restaurant the night before. His eyes had seemed to follow her all around the crowded dining room, and his oily stench had made him stand out like a spot of mold on white linen.

Mandy drew in breath to scream; her hand scrambling across the console for her phone or the gearshift, whichever came first, but he was too fast. With lightning speed, he dove across the seat and slapped a rectangle of duct tape across her mouth. At the same time, he buried his free hand knuckle deep in the thick blonde braid at the base of her skull even as his other hand slid down to her windpipe and began to squeeze.

Mandy's fight instinct kicked in then, and she whipped her head back and forth in an effort to dislodge his hands. His stench, and the oily filth of his unkempt hair, was sickening. She clawed at his eyes, ripped at his skin, but it was no use. The psycho laughed and simply leaned his head back out of her reach.

That's when Mandy began to claw at her own face, attempting to scratch the silver tape off her mouth. It didn't matter. There was no one around to hear her scream even if she could have gotten it off.

She wasn't a quitter, though. Mandy did her best to get her feet out from under the steering column to kick. But he was pressing down on her with his whole weight. She was trapped. Calmly, the psycho took one hand off her throat, doubled up his fist, and hit her so hard the back of her skull struck the driver's side window with an audible *whap!*

Then, he went back to her throat. As his deceptively thin fingers crushed her windpipe, Mandy's grip on reality began to loosen. Tiny strobes flashed inside her skull.

He squeezed even harder; the tips of his fingers disappearing into the flesh of her throat.

At the last second, as her world began to grow dark, a memory flashed through Mandy's mind. She remembered how, as a small girl of six, she had begun to worry about running out of air because if you couldn't see something, how did you know how much of it was left? She *could* see balloons, though. So she had begged her mom to buy several packages of the colorful party staples, which she'd then blown up and stored in her bedroom closet. Her mom humored her. Her older sister, Kami, however, couldn't let a good thing like that go unnoticed.

She had waited until Mandy was out, then she'd tied all the balloons together and attached them to the stop sign on the corner. Mandy had felt so humiliated when she came home from school and saw them. She'd wanted to get them down and put them back in her closet, but she couldn't bring herself to do it. She would have let herself run out of air before giving her sister that satisfaction.

The balloon bouquet had wilted quickly in the hot New Mexico sun.

Now, even as she was dying, Mandy grasped the irony of that memory. She really had run out of air. Her last coherent thought—as the fireworks behind her eyelids exploded in the grand finale—was of those wilting, multicolored balloons.

Chapter Two

Standing in the patch of sunlight, the blond giant smiled crookedly and Beth knew it was John. She rushed forward to embrace him. He was shirtless, wearing nothing but a pair of old cutoffs, his bronze skin glistening with water from the creek. His hair was long, tied back in a ponytail with a knotted length of twine. He was an eighteen-year-old demigod stumbling around the forest in search of his subjects.

He opened his arms at her approach. "Beth." His voice was just as she remembered. She melted into the shelter of his embrace. Her damp, sun-warmed skin met his and she sighed. She was wearing a red bikini top and her own stringy-hemmed cutoffs.

Slowly, she raised her face. The top of her head barely grazed his shoulder. She had to stand on her tip-toes even though he was leaning down—then their lips met, and the brilliant rays of sunlight falling through the pines illuminated his face like that of a saint in a stained-glass window. "Saint John," she laughed.

He laughed with her.

Beth shook her head to clear the memories.

Actually, it wasn't a memory so much as it was an embellished wish. John Stockton was not a figment of her imagination, nor was he a dream-guy. He was a real memory, but it was a childhood memory. A teenage dream. He had been her first crush.

They'd met one summer at Stutter Creek when she and her dad had made their annual vacation trip to their cabin in the mountains. But that was so long ago—the only reason he kept invading her thoughts now was because she'd recently lost her dad. Coming on the heels of her painful divorce from the second love of her life, it had been doubly hard. She had no one to lean on.

Revisiting her memories of John, okay *embellishing* her memories of the boy her Dad had jokingly called Big John because of his height, was just another way of coping with the sudden silence that now enveloped her. Beth knew she'd probably never see John again, except in her dreams.

She lay back in the pillows and drifted away. The over-the-counter sleep aid was beginning to help. This time, her thoughts became a late summer picnic. It was a family outing with her dad and her husband, Sam. Her daughter, Abby, was there, too. She was just a toddler. They were in a soft green park. Mature pre-autumn maple trees shaded a clear pond ringed with soldiers of pampas grass swaying in the breeze. Fish were jumping, birds flitting from branch to branch, and her old crazy quilt was spread with a mini-feast of sandwiches, chips, and soft drinks. To top it all off, there were fat slices of gooey chocolate cake peeking through the transparent plastic lids of Rubbermaid keepers.

In the dream, the sky was clear but for a thin scarf of cirrus clouds draped across the horizon. It was a typical West Texas summer's eve. Beth felt so happy watching Sam, her handsome husband, and her father playing Frisbee near the water. Sam, strong and lithe in his khaki shorts and her dad, boyish as ever in his faded jeans and running shoes, were playing keep-away from her darling, Abby, who was dashing back and forth between them. She was so adorable, twirling and dancing, trying to steal the Frisbee along with a bit of attention, her blond curls and stocky little-girl body clad in pink Osh-kosh overalls and flowery bucket hat.

Sitting on the sidelines, enjoying the air as well as the view, Beth closed her eyes and turned her face up to the westering sun, eager to let the rays coat her skin in their warm liquid silk. What a fantastic day. Her family, her life, everything was perfect. All that was missing was that old song about a wonderful world.

Then, a long black shadow fell across her face blotting out the sun.

She awoke.

The world was inside out; no color, no birds, no pond, just that damn shadow. Her eyes were open, but the room was cave-black except a thin slice of moonlight falling slantwise across the floor from the tall narrow window. Once she saw that slice of light, Beth understood what had happened.

She had finally fallen asleep. But even the sleep-aid hadn't been able to protect her from the dream. Every time she closed her eyes, the blackness came and swallowed her family. She was reminded of her grandmother and how the elderly woman had often suffered from bad dreams and what she'd referred to as "visits."

Beth had always thought the woman was a little off until her grandfather had passed away, that is. Then she had experienced such a clear vision of him standing at the end of her bed, waiting to say goodbye, that she had never doubted her Grandmother's stories again. When she had mentioned it to her Gran, the older woman had simply hugged her and with tears in her eyes, she'd said, "Your momma, she got visits, too."

Beth hadn't really known how to respond to that. Her mom had died of toxemia shortly after Beth was born. When her Gran had passed several years later, Beth had awoken— apparently at the very moment of the elder woman's death from a stroke—to the old John Denver song, "Leaving on a Jet Plane." She awoke hearing the line that gave her an immediate image of her Gran standing out in the hall, luggage in hand, ready to go on a trip. She had a sad look on her sweet old face, as if she hated having to stop by so unexpectedly.

Beth never doubted that it was her Gran, stopping by just like her Granddad had done so many years before. Then, when the same song just happened to be playing on the car radio three days later on the way to the funeral . . . *that* had really convinced her she had been "visited."

"I haven't heard that song in twenty years," Sam had remarked.

She had almost told him about her dream, then. But he had made her feel so silly when she'd told him about her Grandfather stopping by years earlier, that she hadn't bothered to try and talk to him about her Gran's visit.

Beth sighed. None of that was very comforting now. If anything, it made her worry about the awful shadow-dreams even more. And her waking reality was almost as bad. The truth sizzled around her like lightning from a broken sky: her family was gone. She was alone in the dark house because Sam had given up their marriage to pursue happiness with a younger woman. Her father had died from cancer, and Abby, her only child, had eloped with her fiancée just a few short months after Sam moved out.

Beth suspected the elopement was partly Abby's way of coping with the pain of losing her dad and granddad in one fell swoop. And if her new son-in-law hadn't taken a teaching position in Italy, Beth would have been even more thrilled for them. Now, she was just sad. And lonely.

Too bad I can't do something like elope, she thought. *Just run off and start anew. On the other hand, maybe even a minor change of scenery would help.*

Chest tight, she got up and patrolled the silent house. She felt like a ghost in her own life. *What had happened to the last twenty years? Had it been nothing but a dream? Had her whole life been nothing but a dream?* Thoughts, images, and memories roiled through her mind like river rapids, unceasing.

Finally, circuit through the silent house complete, Beth curled up in the living room recliner and turned on the television. At least the noise drowned out the silence. The bluish light of an old movie reminded her of all those Friday nights when she was a child right here in Sandy, Texas sneaking into the midnight living room to watch Shock Theater when her dad had already gone to bed.

She was so exhausted she never even noticed the tiny dots of color that darted here and there around the room. There were dozens of pinpricks of light, every hue and color of the rainbow. Gradually coalescing, they swarmed around her gently, like a delicate diaphanous shawl. Maybe she didn't see them, but perhaps she sensed them for closing her eyes, Beth finally slipped back into sleep, peacefully.

Sunlight woke her the second time. It was just beginning to break through the white eyelet curtains she had made two years ago. Back when the world was right and her life had been populated with loved ones and plans for the future.

She was lying in the center of Abby's soft bed just like she'd done almost every night since the elopement. Though she was certain she had retreated to the recliner at one point, it seemed as if it was growing more and more difficult to tell the dreams from the waking.

Glad to see daylight, Beth untangled herself from the heap of sheets and blankets twisted around her feet. If only it was that easy to untangle the remnants of my life, she thought.

Tears formed at the corners of her eyes. It was such a beautiful morning. The March sunlight falling across the bed was almost as warm and golden as that in her previous dream-park.

Sadness washed over her again. There was no escaping it, no place to hide. Not even sleep could shield her. Her father was gone. Even though she'd known he was terminal, she hadn't been ready. Though he'd suffered horribly, even with the morphine, she still wanted him back. She knew it was selfish; she knew he was better off. But she missed him, needed him. They'd always had such a connection. She'd assumed it was because he'd been her only parent, but maybe it was more than that. Maybe there was something even deeper.

Thinking of her father was bad enough, but then there was Sam, gone but not gone. Betrayer. She didn't want to think about that, refused to think about it. Refused to acknowledge how her entire life had hinged on her husband and her dad.

She clutched the pillow to her face, and screamed out her pain and anger again, and again, and again until her throat was raw and there was nothing left inside but an old riverbed where tears had once flowed.

After a few moments, she felt what she was hoping to feel—empty and dry. But she knew the riverbed wasn't *really* dry. Those tears were still there, like a flash flood waiting for a cloudburst. She was beginning to think they would always be there; that the rest of her life would be rolled out before her on waves of tears.

She had to get out, go somewhere. She recalled her idea of a change of scenery. It was almost her last hope. There was certainly no reason to stay. She had taken a leave of absence from work; she wouldn't have to return until August. Just the thought of preparing her fifth grade classroom for a new group of students made her stomach churn and her chest constrict. In fact, at this moment, she couldn't envision herself *ever* returning to the classroom. It felt as if Mrs. Evans, the teacher, had been replaced by Bethany Brannock, the timid girl of her youth. *How could I have reverted so quickly, so completely?*

She thought the awful nightmares had something to do with her inability to move on. They were every night. In fact, every time she fell asleep, day or night. And they were so real, so depressing, and so frightening.

Stutter Creek, she thought, and she immediately felt a little better.

Struggling from the bed, she pulled a suitcase from her closet and began to stuff it with jeans and T-shirts. Stutter Creek, New Mexico. The place where she and her father had fled after her mother's death so long ago. The place where she had been both a little girl, and later, a young woman.

The place where she had experienced her first real crush.
Big John.

She was positive she would feel better at the Stutter Creek cabin. Already she felt lighter. Just the thought of doing something, instead of simply wallowing in self-pity, made her breathe a tiny bit easier.

It wasn't until she was packed and taking a last minute shower that she let her mind drift back to the latest dream. Even in the stream of warm water cascading down her body, Beth shivered. Images of shadows crept into her mind. She wondered if she would ever sleep normally again. *Would the nightmares continue at the cabin?*

One thing was certain. The nightmares were getting worse here. They were unrelenting. Beth tried to remember what each one was about, but in truth, she was glad when she couldn't. It was always just a feeling of doom, and that thick black shadow that blotted out the sun and seemed to soak up the very air around her.

As she stepped from the shower, she spied the grief counselor's card tucked into the edge of the mirror on her dresser. Cindy, a registered nurse who just happened to be her closest friend, had given her the card only yesterday. She was well aware of the difficulties Beth was experiencing. She'd given her the card in hopes that she could convince her friend to attend a meeting and realize she wasn't alone in her pain.

Beth recalled the feeling of revulsion she'd felt when Cindy had pressed the card into her hand. She didn't want to expose her pain in public. And she certainly didn't want to hear about someone else's trouble.

But that had been yesterday, before the latest bout of nightmares. Now, well, what did she have to lose? She felt like she was nearing the end of her rope. Besides, Cindy said she didn't have to speak, or even give them her name. The hospital referred lots of patients there. She said it was the policy of the group to let folks just sit and listen if that's what made them comfortable. And she promised Beth that if she hated it, she would never mention it again.

Beth looked at the small, non-descript card. Cindy *did* have years of experience with grieving patients. Maybe it was worth a try.

Wrapped in a towel, dripping all over the rug, she picked up her cell phone and tapped in the seven-digit number. She still intended to head for Stutter Creek, but she was half-afraid things would be the same there. *Or even worse.* Perhaps Cindy was right. Maybe talking to a grief expert would ease her mind—and her fears—before she left. *Nothing ventured, nothing gained.* She pulled the towel a bit tighter and listened nervously as the ringing began.

Chapter Three

Danny kept whining that he was cold. Kurt warned him to shut up. What more could the kid want? He had the hat Kurt had taken off a homeless man in the city.

Kurt knew how to keep his son quiet. The first night Danny had spent with him, Kurt had crushed up a prescription pill he'd liberated from his "buddy's" medicine cabinet. He'd sprinkled some of the residue onto a McDonald's hamburger. When Danny complained about the grit, Kurt had grabbed the rest of the burger and tossed it out the car window. The kid never complained about a gritty hamburger again. After that, sleep had taken over, and from then on Danny was seldom awake long enough to register anything.

Kurt was glad the pills made the kid thirsty. That's what kept him in line. He only gave him something to drink when he did what he was told to do.

After Danny had lured Amanda to stop, Kurt had rewarded the kid with a can of lukewarm Pepsi. Danny had downed it quickly. Then he'd dozed off with his back against a live oak. That was just what Kurt intended. It had kept the kid out of Kurt's way.

Danny had been too stoned to notice the lifeless body of Amanda Myers pushed down into the front floorboard. He didn't even wake when Kurt stopped beside the road farther on, wrestled the petite young woman out of the car and heaved her body over the edge of a rough arroyo. Kurt looked at the kid sound asleep in the backseat. He hadn't seen him since he was a baby, but he'd kept tabs on him all along. He knew this was his kid, even if the damn state had taken him away when his mom had gone missing.

Kurt had been in prison for five years, but that had just been for selling drugs; no one had ever officially connected him to his wife's disappearance. As a result, he had never been blocked from knowing his son's whereabouts.

After he was paroled, Kurt had snatched Danny right out of his current foster parents' front yard. The boy had been playing with a friend when Kurt pulled up in a "borrowed" car. It took him only a minute to convince Danny's friend to run home to fetch a Band-Aid for the serious-looking cut on Kurt's hand. Then, when Danny drew closer, to inspect the self-inflicted wound, Kurt had grabbed him. It was almost too easy.

Danny begged to go home. But Kurt had convinced him he was really his daddy and the state had taken him away from him. What could a six year old really know?

After that, the boy hadn't asked to go home anymore. He hadn't asked anything at all. He just did what he was told. An Amber alert had been issued immediately. Kurt guessed someone missed the kid. But he'd heard the news on the car radio. The only thing the other kid had been able to tell them was that Danny had been taken by a man with a cut on his hand.

Kurt entertained himself by ruminating on his plan. He was so furious with the people who had taken away his freedom—especially that hotshot blonde Prosecutor—that he had thought of little else for the past five years.

Now, he had it all figured out. Danny was the bait, and blonde girls were the prey. Pretty little blondes like his missing wife, Sherry, and like that interfering Prosecutor. Kurt didn't want to go back to prison, but someone had to pay for what he'd been through.

His wife had paid as soon as she'd started demanding money from him for things like diapers and formula; now it was time for the Prosecutor to pay. But first, he would show her how powerful he was.

The prison psychiatrist had diagnosed Kurt as a true sociopath. He had absolutely no regard for the rules of society. To Kurt Graham, it had always been about him and no one else.

He had gone through his life totally confused by all the rubbish the system had tried to ingrain into him about compassion, sympathy, and golden rules. None of that made any sense to Kurt. It was survival of the fittest, and that was all. He could spell the word "conscience" but that was as close as he ever got to having one. A conscience only got you in trouble.

He was listed as chronically depressed because he never seemed to fit in. Kurt had been self-medicating long before he got out of junior high school. Alcohol was his first drug of choice. But he'd quickly moved on to others. By the time he was sent to Alternative School for slashing a rival's tires in the school parking lot, he was already an old hand at making his own drugs or selling himself to get the money from someone else.

As soon as he turned eighteen, he dropped out of school and began dealing drugs in earnest. He had just discovered heroin when Sherry moved in. The two of them were in the same shape. She would do anything for drug money. Neither wanted an actual job, or even an actual life. The fact that they were so much alike was what made them comfortable with each other.

It wasn't long before she found out she was pregnant with Danny. And although she loved getting high almost as much as Kurt, she had tried to stay off the harder drugs while she was pregnant. She said she had no intention of being saddled with some brain-damaged brat. Then she had seen a reality show featuring a couple that had paid for a woman's entire pregnancy, delivery, and a bonus. In fact, the couple had been so well to-do, they'd even bought the birth mother a new car.

That's when Sherry had started trying to stay clean. She told Kurt they could get rid of the kid and get a new car, too.

Kurt didn't care about any of that. He was strictly a live for the moment kind of guy. So when Sherry quit partying and bringing in the drugs, or the drug money, he knew something would have to change. Giving up his dope just so she could play mommy was not an option. He'd warned her not to ever get pregnant. Obviously, she'd forgotten their agreement.

It had come as a complete surprise to him when she up and moved in with the couple who were planning to adopt the baby, but when they found out about Sherry's drug history a few months later, they called the whole thing off. In the adoption paperwork, Sherry had checked NO when asked if she'd ever used illegal drugs. They kicked her out.

Kurt was infuriated, but he allowed her to come back to him on the condition she would give the kid up anyway, just as soon as it was born. Sherry had been a very good prostitute. Between the two of them, they'd been able to live just the way he'd always envisioned. Sleep all day, party all night. That's all he wanted. No way he was going to support the both of them plus a kid.

So Sherry had agreed. But once the baby was born Sherry changed. Not only did she stop partying with him, she stopped whoring for him. She became useless.

Danny was almost a year old when Sherry went missing.

By the time Children's Protective Services got involved, even Kurt had forgotten where he'd buried her body.

Someone had alerted CPS that Danny's mother hadn't been seen in a while, and they had paid him a visit, with police in tow, before he could get rid of his lab.

The caseworker had sat across from him in prison and read the report to him. They had discovered Danny in his crib, naked and caked with feces. The back of his head was flat from lying on his back constantly. They said it would take months to heal the bedsores on his malnourished little body.

After hearing the caseworker's report, Carol Jones, the prosecutor, had made it clear that she was making it her mission to get Kurt as much prison time as possible. It was because of her that he'd finally been forced into sobriety for the first time since he was twelve years old.

He didn't like that. Not one little bit. The world was one ugly damn place without the haze of drugs. That's why she had to pay. Kurt had lain on his cot night after night writhing in cold, clear-eyed agony. He'd been stoned all his life for a reason. He didn't like the world when he was sober. Stoned, he could tolerate it, barely.

But she would pay. He would see to that. Carol Jones may have gotten him locked away, but he'd had five years to develop his plan of revenge. She'd made it her mission to get him as much prison time as possible, so Kurt had made it his mission to kill one girl for every year he'd spent behind bars. And he intended to make certain she knew they were all dead because of her. Carol Jones hadn't seen the last of Kurt Graham, not by a long shot.

Chapter Four

Purse gripped tightly in her lap, Beth sat in the folding chair with her ankles crossed and her eyes downcast. She still couldn't believe she was actually attending a grief session. Cindy had offered to come with her, but in the end, Beth thought she would do better with people who *didn't* know she was once the epitome of calm, centered, self-control.

After introducing herself to the group and listening to all of their introductions in return, she said, "All I want to know is whether anyone else has experienced . . . nightmares."

She glanced around the circle of chairs to gauge their reactions, but most of the faces were blank. Some of them looked away or studied their laps or their shoes. So Beth continued, "I expected depression and sadness, maybe even guilt. But these dreams—"

They all began to talk at once. It was as if a dam had suddenly opened. Dalton, the grief counselor, could barely contain the outburst. Apparently, everyone had something to tell.

The lady in the red velour jogging suit said, "When my son died of a drug overdose, I had such vivid nightmares of him wandering lost through the house that I would sometimes awaken to find myself in another room, trying to catch him before he left again . . . it got so bad that my husband started sleeping on the sofa so I wouldn't try to go outside." Obviously holding back tears, she added, "I never walked in my sleep before. Not even as a child."

Beth wanted to ask her how long it went on, but someone else was speaking.

It was the man in the Harley-Davidson tee shirt: "My Sue was killed by a drunk driver. She was a teetotaler, a Christian woman. We prayed together on our knees beside the bed every night before we went to sleep. Every night!" His voice broke as he held out his arms for Beth to see. "I had one tattoo while she was alive," he said. "From my stint in the Navy." Now, both his arms were covered from his wrist to the edge of his short-sleeved tee. "All these tats are memorials to her." He pointed to one that appeared to be some sort of demon. "That thing was in my dreams a lot. I think it wanted me to find that drunk and kill him." His bloodshot eyes were weary, watery. "He only got probation."

He pointed to his other arm. A heavenly angel with blue eyes adorned his forearm. "This is my Sue. She's still with me, too. In my dreams." He looked away, an expression of shame crossing his face. "She wouldn't want me to kill anyone." Then he glanced hard at Dalton as if to say, I know we've resolved this already, but she asked.

Beth wanted to wrap her arms around him, around them both. But another man was speaking, a young man by the name of Jared. "My daughter, Taylor," he whispered. "Leukemia. She was five. I'll never let her go, dreams or no dreams. My wife left me. She couldn't take the screaming. My screaming. The cancer threatens my little girl every night in my dreams. I can't save her. I'll never be able to save her." He dissolved into his chair in tears and Beth *did* go to him, she couldn't help it.

She knelt and placed her arms around him. He was like one of her students in need of comfort. Beth didn't know the group protocol, but she knew the emotion. He held on to her and cried. Someone slipped a chair underneath her as she crouched beside him, and then she knew it was okay. She knew she would be okay, too.

If this poor man can keep on fighting, then so can I, she told herself. It isn't like I lost a child. At least mine happened in the correct order: parents are supposed to die before children. Millions of people experience it everyday.

Finally, that one simple fact gave her a tremendous measure of comfort. Just knowing she wasn't alone.

She called Cindy on the way home. "You were right. I'm not going crazy. It turns out that everything I'm experiencing is perfectly normal. In fact, Dalton said he'd be more surprised if I *wasn't* having bad dreams. You know, seeing as how the two most important men in my life deserted me, so to speak. And then Abby—I keep dreaming about my little blond girl disappearing—well, she basically has, hasn't she?"

"Yes," Cindy agreed. "Italy is a long distance from here. I'm just glad you're feeling better. Are you sure you're ready to be totally alone, though?"

Beth assured her she was. Then she went straight home and loaded up the car.

She locked up the house and was almost overwhelmed with a tremendous feeling of melancholy. There was no one to know if she returned or not. The click of the deadbolt on the front door was very loud in the tiled entry. She gave herself a little shake to dislodge the blues, and then she turned off the kitchen radio, straightened her spine, marched out to the garage and slung her purse into the passenger seat of the '69 Camaro. It had been her graduation gift from her father so many years earlier—a classic, even then—and they had spent many happy hours together as he taught her to care for it and keep it running. He always joked that she was the son he'd never had.

After a stop at the grocery store, she was finally on the road.

Streaking through the night like a flash of blue lightning on wheels, she glanced at the speedometer. Eighty. Slowly, she eased her foot off the Camaro's accelerator. Her dad always said she had lead in her heel and ball bearings in her butt. The memory made her smile, but it also made her recall how many times the two of them had made this trip together.

She wiped away a sneaky tear sliding down her cheek, but it was too late. Once the tears got started, more followed. And more. And still more, until she was blubbering and leaking like a forgotten faucet.

Everywhere she went, everything she did, triggered memories of her father, or her husband, or her daughter. She felt abandoned, a middle-aged orphan. The thought did not comfort her.

It occurred to Beth that the best part of her life might now be over. Both of her parents were gone, her only child was living in another country, and her spouse of a quarter century had simply tossed her out with the trash. She tried to combat it, but suddenly she was completely overcome. She felt old, alone, and useless.

The blubbering turned to sobbing, which turned to shaking, and then the shaking became so bad that her foot jerked on and off the accelerator. She tried to keep it steady, but trying only made it worse. She was on the verge of hysteria.

The on and off motion of her foot made the little car buck like a mechanical bull in need of a tune up. Anyone seeing the car juddering down the highway would swear the driver was three-sheets-to-the-wind. Or having some sort of medical emergency.

Beth began to wonder if she *was* having some sort of breakdown. Maybe the grief group had been a bad idea. All those emotions . . .

The shoulder of the highway wouldn't stay put. Every few seconds, she would veer onto the shoulder and then back onto the highway. Her tires would kick up loose gravel and she would yank the steering wheel back toward the road. When she couldn't seem to control it, Beth began to worry that she would overreact and wrench the wheel so sharply that it would cause her to roll.

That's what finally helped her get her emotions in check. She took a deep breath. Her foot stopped spasming on the accelerator, her sobs tapered off to hiccups, and the hiccups replaced the shakes, at least for the most part.

Frightened at the ferocity of her mini-breakdown, Beth reached for the bottle of water she'd bought at the grocery just before leaving town. Her throat was parched from all the sobbing, but the bottle had fallen to the floor during her wild, bucking ride.

She checked her rearview mirror and prepared to stop and look for the bottle. Applying the brakes and downshifting carefully, Beth glanced in the rearview one more time. These gravelly shoulders could be dangerous. But she really needed a drink of water. Hopefully, she'd gotten the hysteria out of her system. She felt guilty for falling apart. She also felt guilty for thinking it was easier to lose a parent than a child or a spouse like some of the others in the grief group. Then she felt guilty for even presuming to know how horrible it must be to lose a child or a spouse. In short, she just felt damn guilty.

Dalton had said what she was feeling was natural, called it "survivor's guilt." She'd heard of that, but it had always been in relation to things like war or plane crashes. Beth hoped the counselor knew what he was talking about, because he had said it would get better. He said not to lose hope, because, *eventually*, it would get better.

At last, she was completely stopped. The sound of her tires crunching on gravel was very loud in the still night.

She pulled out the little knob to engage the Camaro's emergency flashers just as her fingers found the smooth curve of the plastic water bottle under the seat. She opened the screw top and took a long fluid gulp. Then she rolled the still-cool bottle across her burning cheeks. Crying always made her face flame and her nose stuff up. She felt calmer but still miserable. Rather than being a comfort, it was as if she'd just realized that she had stopped in the middle of nowhere, alone.

It's like a badly written soap opera, she thought. No one should have to go through this alone. *Should have had more children, then maybe one of them would still be nearby.* But of course, she didn't fault her daughter for returning to her own life after the funeral. In fact, she had encouraged it. Beth couldn't stand to see the hurt in her grown-up little girl's eyes each time her father was mentioned. Seeing him at the funeral had brought it all to the surface again. Out of necessity, and perhaps a healthy dose of self-preservation, the hurt she herself felt had been put on hold.

Maybe that's what is coming out now—the pain of seeing Sam again. Just seeing him sitting there in the pew on the other side of Abby, knowing that his young lover was waiting for him at home, had caused a marrow-deep ache that came from the knowledge that this, burying a parent, was what the vows they had taken had been all about. But that didn't matter to Sam. *She* no longer mattered to Sam.

Closing her eyes, Beth leaned back in her car seat and took several deep breaths to make sure the panic had truly subsided. The outside air was much cooler than it had been when she'd left West Texas at lunchtime. Back home, on the edge of the Chihuahuan desert, it had been seventy-one degrees, even in January.

But now she was nearing the Sacramento Mountains of New Mexico. There was a threadbare cover of snow on the shoulder of the highway, much deeper in the roadside ditches. The thin coverlet became a fluffy comforter across the darkening fields, quilting the foliage beneath the snow into patchwork shapes of light and dark. The air was moist, but no moisture was currently falling. Night was falling. She had forgotten how quickly darkness took hold in the mountains.

As the moon rose, the snow began to shine. It was beautiful, shimmering faintly, softly reflecting both the scant moonlight and the Camaro's headlights. It made the entire countryside glimmer like a mirror wrapped in white silk.

Beth screwed the lid back onto the water bottle and rolled it gratefully across her burning cheeks and forehead one last time before placing it back into the drink holder. Then she opened her eyes and looked directly into the looming face of a small boy in an old-fashioned cap.

She screamed.

He was standing near the front of the Camaro like a little ghost, staring dully into her eyes from beneath the brim of his slouchy, too large hat.

Her hands flew up to her face. She wanted her right hand to engage the gearshift, but she couldn't quite make it do that. Both hands were frozen over her eyes. They would not obey her.

The boy tapped the passenger's side window. Beth looked; she had no choice. His face was almost touching the glass.

She might've screamed again, but there was no air. Her breath was stuck somewhere in the back of her throat. She stared into his eyes.

The boy was pale, tear-streaked, and filthy. A breeze toyed with the damp fringe of hair sticking out from under the edge of his cap. As she watched, a drop of moisture slid to the end of his upturned nose and hung there for what seemed an eternity. When it fell onto his upper lip, he didn't even seem to notice.

Squeezing her eyes shut, Beth took a deep breath, opened them, and then leaned over to manually roll down the window—but he had disappeared. From behind her came the lights of an eighteen-wheeler.

Had she really seen a boy? She leaned over as far as possible with the stick shift digging into her side, but she couldn't see any tracks. The snow was too thin and patchy.

The truck's headlights lit up her rearview mirror. They grew larger and larger as she watched, like twin orbs caught in the glass. She reached down and felt the little knob below the steering wheel to make certain her emergency flashers were still on. She was certain that would get the truck to stop. Then they could search the bar ditch together—no child should be alone on the highway. Perhaps someone was hurt down there. Maybe their car slid off in the ditch or something.

But the truck driver blew one short note on his air horn, and then he roared past and was gone. The lights outlining his trailer looked like a carnival.

Beth was stunned. *Now what? Get out and search by myself?* Intuition said no. There was something altogether wrong about a child that appeared and disappeared like an apparition. *Perhaps he hadn't been there at all,* her mind whispered. *Hadn't the lady in the grief group suffered hallucinations? Could I have been that distraught?*

She rolled the window up and locked both doors. Icy fear gripped her. She looked all around, but there were no cars, no houses, nothing. Why would the boy have gone away if he needed help? Surely he knew she would help him. *What if someone is hurt? Or what if he was being kidnapped and he'd briefly gotten loose? Or what if it was a trap?* Last year she'd seen an MSN article about a man who had put a baby carrier beside the road in an attempt to lure women into stopping.

She pulled out her cell phone and checked for a signal.

No service.

Not surprising this close to the mountains.

Suddenly, Beth made a decision. She rammed the gearshift lever into first and stepped on the gas. Fishtailing back onto the road, she shifted up to second, and then third, keeping her eyes trained on the highway ahead. She knew the boy was no longer there, but what if he appeared while she was moving? What if he was somehow hanging onto the car like that old urban legend about the killer with a hook? What if he appeared while she was *driving?*

She thought if that happened, it might be the end. It would send her right over the edge of sanity into the cavern of insanity. One hand crept back up to her face. She was afraid the boy wasn't human. His face had seemed so pale, almost translucent. A little phantom.

No, no, no. It was her *mind*. It was playing tricks on her. That had to be it.

Staring straight ahead, she pressed the gas harder and harder, shifting up into fourth without even thinking, years of experience guiding her.

Beth began to feel like an idiot, a complete, dyed-in-the-wool idiot. *Did I fall asleep while driving? Did I pass out? Maybe Dalton was wrong; maybe I'm stark raving mad!* She drove on, running on instinct and adrenalin, terrified that she'd seen a real boy, even more terrified that she hadn't.

Finally, her rational mind began to reassert itself. *There is no way that was a ghost, and I'm not crazy, just emotional.*

Common sense kept talking. *What if the boy was real? What if he was lost, or had been in some sort of accident? What if one of those things accounted for the unearthly glow of his pale skin and the flat, shineless cast of his eye? What if he was really there and she was leaving him to die?*

Dad, she thought, I sure wish you were here.

She scoured the sides of the road for some clue, or at least a sign of some sort.

Dark wintry trees blurred past. The moon coated her hood with white, and the wind whistled through the tiny gaps around the windows. She thought about the radio, maybe there was a report about a missing boy, but when she turned it on, all she got was static. No radio, no phone. It was as if she had entered the Twilight Zone.

All at once, she got a calming image of her father. She had never seen him panic. She tried to imagine what he would do, and suddenly, it was as if he were there with her. Beth imagined a whiff of wood smoke, the smell she associated with him and his love of camping and hiking. She felt better. Stronger. Once again, she glanced into the mirror. Beth never noticed the tiny colored lights that glittered briefly near the corner of her eye. She was watching for a mile marker.

Carefully, she picked up her cell phone and tried to call 911 again. She could feel the adrenalin leaving her body. She vowed to keep trying to call until she reached the DPS. They would check it out. She would tell them she thought she had seen a child. She didn't have to admit that she thought it could've been a ghost.

Her cell beeped.

Still no signal.

Damn.

A child.

She slowed and downshifted to execute a u-turn. *There's no way I can drive on if there's a chance that child was real and not a figment of my tortured imagination.* She leaned over and checked the lock on the passenger side door.

Surely it wasn't a real boy. I would rather it be an apparition, or even a hallucination . . . anything but a child alone beside a snow-filled bar ditch.

If I can't find him, she decided, I'll drive in to the next town and locate the Police Station. I can't take a chance that there might be a real little boy out there, alone.

Chapter Five

Cursing the big rig, Kurt yanked Danny back down into the ditch. It had been simple to throw the kid, and himself, down into the fluffy white drift of snow. He had only pulled off the road into the trees to grab a few minutes shuteye after putting a good distance between himself and Pine River. But when he awoke, the car had been completely covered in a thin shroud of snow.

He thought the crunch of tires on gravel might be what had awakened him, and when he'd seen that the driver of the silvery blue Camaro was a woman, alone, he'd sent Danny over to check her out.

Amanda had been such an easy target. He couldn't wait to try it again—even if this one wasn't on his list.

The list—and more importantly, the plan—was the thing that had kept him going while he was in prison. It was all he thought about. He wasn't even going to allow himself to get wasted again until he had completed his plan. Kurt knew he was smarter than everyone else. Now he was about to prove it.

As soon as he had gotten out of prison, he'd gone to work on the plan. The first part had been easy: finding the girls. Now that he was sober, they seemed to be everywhere, and with the help of certain "business" associates, they were extremely easy to locate. One of his "businessmen" from Albuquerque—Dave, the cokehead with the penchant for young women—even gave Kurt access to his computer dating site. These were not hookers masquerading as dates. Nope. This was an honest-to-God dating website made up of fresh-faced college girls. It encompassed most of New Mexico.

That's where he'd found Amanda's picture. She was young and blonde. He thought she would fit perfectly into his plan.

He immediately contacted her through the site's message board, and they began to chat. He could be quite charming when he wanted to. On the computer he quoted Rumi and Deepak Chopra, two authors of poetry and enlightenment whose books he'd flipped through while he was in prison.

Amanda seemed to be somewhat smitten. He made sure he didn't come across as just another beer-swilling college jerk. Kurt was certain she saw those all the time on campus, or in her job as a nighttime waitress at the Water House Bar & Grill.

Amanda had agreed to meet him at the mall. Kurt knew she was being cautious, insisting on meeting in a public place. But that was okay. She seemed to be somewhat smitten.

There was only one thing. She would be looking for someone tall and lanky, with streaky, sun-bleached hair and glasses. She would be looking for the "businessman" he had met in prison. The one who would agree to anything if it involved free drugs, which is exactly how Kurt had convinced him to hand over the password to his dating profile.

When the man she was expecting didn't show up for their rendezvous, Mandy had simply headed back to the dorm. Kurt suspected she had soothed her injured self-esteem with a pint of ice cream the way Sherry used to do when she got mad or wasted.

He wondered if she had gone straight in and deleted the dating site that had caused her to humiliate herself by sitting alone in the mall food court for almost an hour, waiting for Mr. Wonderful. He hoped that she had. It would just be that much harder for the police to trace later. But again, he didn't care. By the time they got that far in their investigation, he planned to be hundreds of miles away.

In the food court, Kurt had sat at a different table, watching her closely. She'd been easy to pick out of the crowd. She'd done exactly what he'd asked her to do when they had agreed to meet. Just like a little sheep, he thought. Or a lamb to the slaughter. And who would have believed her photo looked exactly like it should have? It wasn't made up to look better the way some girls did when posting on those sites.

He'd had no problem following her back to her car, and then to the dorm. No one noticed a short, scruffy-looking guy on a college campus. He certainly wasn't the tall, blond businessman Mandy had been looking for.

That evening, when she'd left for work, he'd followed her then, too. It had only taken a few days to get a handle on her routine. Then it was easy to find a deserted spot to station Danny. Just for fun, he'd even gone into The Water House Bar & Grill and requested her section. Being that close to someone he planned to kill was the most exciting thing he'd ever done. Not that it was the first time he'd taken someone's life; it was more exciting this time because he was still in the planning stage. There was definitely something to be said for anticipation. Besides, for once, he'd been stone cold sober.

Kurt couldn't believe how easy it was to find the girls to put on his five-year list. Yep, finding them was the easy part. But he didn't get them all through the dating site. That would make connecting the dots way too easy for the cops. Instead, he also checked out Facebook. Lots of girls actually had their work places listed right on their profiles. That's where he had found his first victim, Sherylyn. Amanda was victim number two.

Kurt felt as if he had been invited to a smorgasbord each time he logged on to his friend's computer. A lot had changed in the few short years since he'd gone to prison. And he hadn't even visited Craigslist yet. But he planned to, one of these days.

So far, it had all been very simple. Once he knew where his target worked, all Kurt had to do was watch them for a few days to learn their routines. And the rest, as they say, would become history.

Of course, while he was waiting to carry out his plan— finding the girls and watching them—he had to have cash. But there were so many ways to make money if one wasn't afraid of getting his hands dirty.

His needs were very simple: cash for food, cigarettes, and drugs. He could get all three by trading favors on the street. He'd never been averse to trading sex for drugs, in fact, that was one area where his wiry build, ice blue eyes, and high cheekbones served him well. Certain types of men would automatically assume he was for sale just because he was somewhat delicate looking. Often, they found out the hard way that there was nothing delicate about him. But he was definitely for sale.

Kurt didn't want drugs yet, though. Not for himself. That would come later, after his entire plan had been carried out and he was ready to kick back and relax on some South American beach. For now, his drug of choice was murder. The street drugs he acquired were strictly for bargaining.

After he'd snatched Danny and worked out his list of girls, Kurt was finally ready to implement the rest of his plan.

He'd thought this part out, too. When he was done, he would send a note to the news media and to Carol Jones, the prosecutor, telling her where to find the bodies so that she could see that even though she may have won in court, he was the winner in real life. Once he'd made his point, and the bodies were piled up at her proverbial doorstep, then he might be ballsy enough to follow her home and learn her routine. Being a woman, he was certain she too would stop for a little boy standing beside a lonely road. But that wasn't a given. That would be like the cherry on top of the sundae.

Tonight, though, he had to put a few more miles on his buddy Dave's old car. He'd slept longer than he anticipated, and he wanted to make it to his mountain hideout before morning. It was very near the place where his next victim worked.

He'd located it with the use of Google Maps. He couldn't believe how easy everything was now. And since the freaky old broad in the Camaro had sped away, he didn't even have to give Danny a reward.

Chapter Six

Completely exhausted, Beth was thankful it was only a few more miles to the cabin. If it hadn't been, she might have turned around and gone home. Except home—the beautiful split-level for which they had scrimped and saved and finally paid off—was the place she was desperately trying to avoid. It hurt to walk through rooms she had once thought of as sanctuary, and which were now somehow worse than just empty.

Even sweet little Ladybug was gone. Ladybug was the tiny mixed breed stray that had hung around the elementary school one day. The office was going to call the pound to come and pick her up, but Beth took pity on her, took her home and placed an ad in the paper. No one claimed her so Ladybug simply stayed. Unfortunately, she hadn't lasted long. The little dog was elderly. But at least she had died knowing she was loved and wanted. Beth thought that was what the little thing had been looking for. In a way, she felt like Ladybug now; tossed aside when she was no longer young and cute.

She supposed comparing herself to a stray dog was sort of silly, but she'd always had an affinity for animals. It was as if they knew she was trustworthy. As a child, she'd always been the one bringing home the stray dog or cat.

Beth wished the little dog were still with her. Hard to believe she's been gone over a year now. If not, she would be right here beside me, offering her own brand of doggy comfort. Perhaps when I get home I'll adopt another dog. Or just sit out on the front porch and wait for one to adopt me.

The turn to the driveway of the cabin appeared suddenly through the trees, taking her by surprise the way it always did, even though she had been watching for the opening for two miles.

It was late now, full dark, but the moon reflecting off the snow lit up the landscape. It made it easy for her to see that the driveway was undisturbed except for the tracks of a small animal, a fox perhaps, going from one side of the yard to the other.

Beth was so grateful that her father had held on to the small cabin. It felt more like home now than the split-level back in Sandy.

The short distance from the road to the cabin ended in a circle drive that led right up to the front door. Beth turned off the engine and listened to the silence for a moment. Then she stepped from the car carefully, feeling around with her toe for ice beneath the snow. Apparently, the weather had been mild. The snow was fresh, no frozen hazard lurking underneath.

Holding fast to her key ring, Beth made the few steps from the car to the covered porch. She found the cabin key by feel. It was a skeleton key. She had taken it from her father's key ring and placed it on hers shortly after the funeral. It was like a talisman. It made her feel better.

Her dad had possessed quite a dramatic sense of humor. He had found the ancient lock interesting, so he'd had an expert repair it when they had first bought the ramshackle cabin back when she was just a little girl.

The porch was inhabited by shadows, some shallow, near the steps, some much deeper, where the porch met the wall. In places some were so black they seemed to be poured on, as though a bucket of ink had been splashed across the front of the cabin. She wondered about the boy again.

Once she had driven out of the closed-in valley, up a bit higher on the mountain, she had finally gotten through to the

DPS via 911. A trooper by the name of Tad Donaldson had met her at the mile marker nearest where the incident had occurred. He'd been very interested in her story. Apparently, a boy had been kidnapped in Albuquerque a couple of weeks earlier.

Beth felt terrible. Together, she and Trooper Donaldson had driven back along her route, stopping to check every stand of trees on the east side of the highway. They found nothing out of the ordinary. Unfortunately, a fresh, heavy, snow had begun to fall before Beth had even got out of the valley.

After a couple of hours of searching, the trooper had taken her report and her cell number. He'd also noted the location of the Stutter Creek cabin.

She'd listened as the trooper contacted dispatch and told them to relay the description of the boy to all local law enforcement offices in the city, county, and state.

But Beth could tell he was beginning to doubt her story. After searching for a while, Beth noticed the trooper wasn't making eye contact with her anymore. She didn't really blame him. It was just too farfetched. How could a child be there one moment and not the next?

She was beginning to doubt it, herself. When Trooper Donaldson asked her if she'd been under any stress recently, she broke down and told him she was going to the cabin specifically to get away from the sorrow of losing her father and her husband.

He'd nodded sagely. Then he had regaled her with stories of the many highway accidents he had worked that occurred simply because an exhausted driver swerved to avoid something in the road—like a dancing stove, or a peacock in a top hat. And these folks were not under the influence of anything, he'd said. They were just guilty of operating a motor vehicle on too little sleep, or under too much stress, or both.

Now, taking a deep breath, Beth slid the key into the lock and turned. It creaked loudly, just as it was supposed to. Her dad had adored that sound. A love of spooky books and movies had been one of the many things they had shared. Campfire stories had been another.

Toward the end of their marriage, Sam had confessed that he'd often felt jealous of her dad. "I could never compete with him," he'd told her, after she had caught him in another one of his lies.

Her friend, Cindy, had chalked it up to Sam trying to shift some of his own guilt onto Beth. But thinking back . . . hadn't she seen signs that he sometimes felt left out on occasions when they were all together? Their daughter, Abby, certainly hadn't felt excluded. When she was growing up, she was the light in her Grampa's eyes. Every weekend, the two of them were together. Just like when Beth, herself, was a girl.

Sam had never complained about that. If he was jealous of Tom's relationship with his granddaughter, it never showed. Usually, he would even join them on the camping and fishing trips. Especially when Beth couldn't go. She had thought it was evidence that he had melded to her dad the same way she had. The way Big John Stockton had that one magical summer.

But apparently, she'd been wrong. About everything. Her husband's treachery had come at her like a train out of a black tunnel. Though she may have felt the rumblings, she had willingly believed his lies and excuses right up to the day she had come home from school early and found him and his young lover in her own bed. She didn't think the pain would ever end, but she hadn't really had time to process all the hurt because that's when her dad's health took a nosedive. Within months, they were both gone. All of them, actually. First, Sam, then Abby, then her dad.

She shook her head as if to physically clear away the memories the way one would shake a dust mop to get rid of the dust. She flipped a switch and was relieved when light filled the small room. True to form, her dad had made sure the gasoline-powered generator was full and in good repair the last time he'd left the cabin. He had come up here alone after Abby married and moved to Italy. Beth knew he was happy for Abby, having found the love of her life, but she thought that maybe he had also come to grieve the loss of his best camping companion. By then, he'd known his time was getting short, so he'd jokingly told everyone he was going to the cabin to pray for great-grandchildren to be born quickly.

"I'll fly to Italy and personally feed them oysters if that's what it takes!" he had boasted. But everyone knew he hated to fly. It was a huge family joke that was told every time anyone had to make a trip.

When he and her mother had flown to Niagara Falls for their honeymoon, the plane had experienced electrical problems and had to return to the airport. Everyone had sat quietly while an electrician was brought on board to fix the problem.

After an hour the electrician packed up his tools and departed. That's when the captain had jovially announced that he thought they had the problem fixed and they would soon be underway.

"You think the problem is fixed?" her dad had asked incredulously. Then, so the story goes, he had collected his new bride along with their new carry-on luggage and several dirty looks, and he'd gotten them the hell off the plane.

Half an hour later, Tom and his new bride, Carrie, had been driving up the interstate in a rented Lincoln Continental listening to Boston on cassette and talking about where they would stop for the night.

They'd finally made it to Niagara Falls, but by the time they got there, they had experienced a whole blissful week of driving and stopping and seeing the United States of America. He said they had spent only one gorgeous day and night in Niagara before gathering up the checked baggage that had made the plane trip without them. They'd lost their huge honeymoon-suite deposit for being so late, but he claimed they had never regretted one minute of the trip.

Her dad always said that was the way everything about his married life had been: absolutely no regrets. They were married only three years before Beth was born and her mom perished from toxemia.

Pushing her brown hair off her forehead, Beth vowed to cheer up. Her dad had managed when her mom died, and it would be letting him down if she couldn't pull herself up out of the mire now. Besides, he'd always assured her that there was life after death. They hadn't been churchgoers so to speak, but he'd instilled in her a deep respect for God, the creator of all things, and time and again he'd assured her that her mom was with God and the angels. And, one day, they would all be there, reunited.

Beth sighed. She believed everything he'd taught her; she'd taught Abby the same things—but it was just so hard to accept that he was gone. Now this . . .

Exhaustion had to be the reason for the hallucination on the highway. That had to be it. She blinked and her eyes were gritty from lack of sleep. She adjusted the propane-fueled heater that would have the little cabin toasty in no time, and she also took a moment to light the fire her dad had laid in the river rock fireplace. Another one of his rules: always lay the fire and have the kindling nearby before you leave.

Beth was so glad for that little habit that she made a silent vow to always do the same when she left the cabin, even if she wasn't sure when she would be able to return. It was like the rule her Aunt Clare had about scissors in the kitchen—more valuable than any knife, always have them handy.

Now, having warmth and light, Beth stooped to turn on the water. The shutoff valve was under the kitchen sink. That pipe and valve were heavily insulated, as were all the pipes in the cabin. Nevertheless, it was always shut off upon leaving. Nothing worse than coming up for a vacation and finding everything flooded and ruined. It hadn't happened to them, but she had seen it in the nearest neighbor's cabin two miles down the road. She never wanted to see that again. Things molded quickly here in the rainy spring.

Finally, Beth made the short trip out to the car to bring in the groceries she'd brought. She wasn't sure how long she was going to stay, but she thought it was time she did something to help herself stop grieving over someone who no longer wanted her.

All in all, she seemed set. Though she had never actually stayed at the cabin by herself for more than one or two nights, usually while waiting for her dad or Sam to get off work and join her, or for Abby to finish a college class, this seemed to be the only place where she could really rest and get away from the awful memories of a life that had turned out to be nothing but an illusion. Nothing but a fractured fairytale.

Chapter Seven

John had only been home for a couple of weeks, just long enough to get some of the dust swept out of the cabin and the broken windows replaced. He was glad he'd had the forethought to put a metal roof on his tiny home. Otherwise, he felt sure the whole thing would be open to the elements by now. He eyed the back of the house critically. Was there room for a studio? He unpacked his easel and oils carefully, his sketchbooks too. Sometimes, they were the only things that had kept him sane while he was overseas on assignment.

He stopped unloading his new furniture from the truck just as Turk came crashing through the underbrush. The huge Anatolian Shepherd was so excited to see his master that he stood on his hind legs and placed his giant paws on the big man's chest. John knew on anyone else, the paws would have landed on shoulders, but he stood six feet four inches tall in his stocking feet. That meant with his lug-soled boots on, he was easily six and a half feet.

"Hey, mutt," he mock-scolded. "What happened to your manners? Did you miss me that much? Next time maybe you'll come when I call. You missed a trip into town. I had to load this new furniture all by myself." The entire time he was speaking, John was rolling the big dog's head back and forth, his grip on the thick mane of fur tender and careful. He'd rescued the Shepherd from his very last private bodyguard assignment in Kazakhstan.

John's employer was only one of the American contractors responsible for bringing ready-made building supplies to the petroleum-rich country, and they moved from place to place quickly. It was nothing for them to put up an office complex in a matter of days, nor was it unusual for them to have to vacate said complex just as quickly. That's why the company security was so necessary.

The last time, when the government liaison had said it was time to vacate, John and his crew had made a last minute sweep through the complex to make sure everyone was out. That's when a stray bullet came through the window and took out most of Turk's right shoulder.

Turk was always with them, he took his job as protector very seriously. Just like any good law enforcement K-9, he had been trained to take down suspects, and search through buildings.

There were a few differences between Turk and regular German police dogs, however. For starters, his breed originated in Turkey. They were originally bred for guarding livestock and they loved their jobs. In fact, if they didn't have something to guard, they could become aggressive and hard to handle.

But that wasn't the only difference between Anatolian Shepherds and most other guard dogs. Size was their most defining feature. That's what made them so intimidating. Standing nearly thirty inches at the shoulder, Turk weighed just shy of one hundred fifty pounds. His short, thick fur was the color of buckskin, his ears and muzzle were black, and his lively brown eyes bespoke an intelligence far superior to that of the average dog, police or otherwise. When happy or standing at attention, his long fuzzy tail curled over his back like a question mark, as if to say, "Okay, I'm ready. What next?" Turk was always game for anything. If unregistered dogs had middle names, Courage would have been his.

Back in Kazakhstan, in the chaos of the battle that had sprung up outside the office complex, the smart thing would have been to leave the injured dog and run for the chopper. Smart, however, didn't factor in the pleading brown eyes that fastened on John's as the dog began dragging itself toward the landing pad. Turk knew the drill, when the shooting starts, it's time to bug out, just like they'd done so many times before.

With only a split second to decide, John had scooped up the bloody mass of bone and fur on the run. He'd then grabbed a coworker's hand and would have pulled him from the open chopper door if he hadn't helped to hoist the big Shepherd inside first. John jumped in when the bird was already two or three feet off the ground. Fortunately, there was a private doctor at the company headquarters who owed John a huge favor—John had been his bodyguard on several occasions. He took care of the wound and made sure the dog was comfortable on the company's private jet. Then he gave John a giant-size bottle of canine antibiotics and wished him luck.

Now, John let Turk down gently, making sure not to jar the still-stiff shoulder. It would probably always require cortisone shots to keep from freezing up, but John thought it was a small price to pay for such a remarkably close call.

With one more pat on the big dog's head, he turned to finish unloading the truck. In addition to a new generator and refrigerator, John had also splurged on a California King mattress set, a new sofa, and an extra-large recliner. Everything he'd had before had been ruined by mice and squirrels. He regretted not paying someone to look after the place while he was gone, but it was never his intention to be away so long.

It was still hard for him to believe he had been away from this place for over twenty years. It felt as if he'd never left. The intervening years had passed so quickly, it was as if they belonged to someone else. As if he'd been someone else, perhaps.

Recruited for private security duty right out of a six year stint in the Army, he'd spent the majority of those twenty years moving from place to place, always looking over his shoulder in his effort to protect whomever he was working for at the time. It had been quite an exciting life.

He'd never had time to settle down. Actually, he'd never found any reason to settle down. But, the years abroad had changed him. He'd vowed to make Kazakhstan his final assignment, especially after he'd nursed the loyal Shepherd back to health. It was as if Turk was the sign he'd been looking for, the sign that it was time to try living a normal life for a change.

John chuckled as he remembered how much red tape he'd had to go through to get Turk into the States. He reached down to ruffle the broad head again, but the dog was standing off near the edge of the yard, looking at him.

"What?" he asked, as though the dog could answer. He automatically scanned the perimeter of the clearing, immediately alert for anything out of the ordinary. Turk didn't bark or whine, he just stood looking at John, obviously wanting something.

He wrestled the new, Indian-blanket-inspired sofa onto the dusty porch and strode to where Turk appeared to be waiting patiently. Before he reached him, however, the Shepherd turned and disappeared into the forest.

John was dumbfounded. Turk was usually so well behaved, like a furry shadow at his heels. In fact, today was the first time he had ever seen the animal have an original thought, other than trying to drag himself to the chopper after the shooting. But, of course, that had just been self-preservation.

He had never acted like this before. Come to think of it, maybe the dog had never been in a pine forest before. Probably wants me to check out a chipmunk or something,

John thought, trailing along with a bemused expression on his face.

Chapter Eight

In her bright, cheerful living room, Barbara Myers was beginning to worry. Truthfully, she had spent all evening worrying. Now at nearly midnight, she was beginning to panic. The television was on, but Barb couldn't concentrate on anything, not even Leno, her favorite talk show host.

Something wasn't right. Amanda had never failed to call when she said she would. Barb was expecting to hear all about her midterms.

She had spent a very restless evening, dialing the number of Mandy's little green cell phone, hoping against hope that she had just left it at the dorm or let the battery run down, or even lost it, anything. Finally, she could stand it no longer. She had called Kami. Her older daughter immediately insisted they call The Water House Bar & Grill in Pine River to see if Mandy was at work.

Barbara clasped her hands together tightly. "Are you sure, Kami? I wouldn't want to get her in trouble with her boss."

"This is Mandy, Mom, not me," Kami said. "Mandy wouldn't simply forget to call you. Something's wrong—if you don't want to call her boss, I will. Just give me the number." And just like that, it was decided.

In The Water House Bar & Grill, Myra listened to Mr. Pope, the manager, speaking to someone on the phone. She thought it was Mandy's mom.

He was telling the person that Mandy had picked up some boy and hadn't shown up for work. Then he stated that behavior like that would not insure Mandy's job no matter how out of character it seemed.

As he was reading the caller the riot act, Myra was on her way out the door, her shift finally over. She had worried about Mandy all evening. Now, she whipped out her own cell and tried calling Mandy's phone one more time—for good measure. But she got nothing, not even voice mail.

Myra stood there, chewing the cuticle around her thumbnail, one hand twirling the dark ponytail that had slipped almost completely free of its elastic band. "Mr. Pope," she said, reaching toward him hesitantly. "May I speak to Mandy's mom?"

Her boss turned even more crimson than usual. "Not now, Myra. Besides, this isn't her mom, it's her sister." He glowered down at her and she wished she could slip out the door or melt into the floor.

"Please?" She straightened her spine as she spoke. "I—I think something is wrong. Mandy would never ditch work . . ."

Mr. Pope looked at the tiny girl again. "Myra, right?" he asked.

She nodded, pulling her sweater around herself protectively. Myra was the newest employee. She hadn't spoken directly to the "big" boss since her initial interview except to answer yes sir or no sir.

Finally, he seemed to realize what it must have taken for her to speak up. He held out the phone.

Myra could hear a woman's voice saying, "Hello, hello? Are you there?"

Taking a deep breath, she responded, "Hello, I'm a friend of Mandy's here at the Water House, I think something has happened . . ." Then she told Kami everything that Amanda had said on the phone. She also told her she would go to the police station if necessary. Her voice trembled as she spoke.

After they hung up, Kami called the Pine River Police Department. The tremble in the other girl's voice frightened her badly.

The officer on phone-duty took down her name, and Mandy's name. Then he advised her to make the trip to the city the next day if they still hadn't heard from Mandy. "We can't report an adult as missing until twenty-four hours have passed—unless we have extenuating circumstances. "

Kami relayed the conversation Myra had told her about, especially the part about Mandy picking up a boy on the highway. That seemed to make him take her a bit more seriously.

"You say she was on her way to work when this occurred?" he asked.

"Yes," Kami replied. She exhaled, relieved that he was beginning to see the urgency. "And she hasn't been heard from since."

After a few beats of silence, the officer said, "And I don't suppose she was in the habit of picking up stray men, er, boys. Right?"

Exasperated, Kami blew her bangs out of her eyes and forced herself to remain calm before she answered. "She was valedictorian of her class, first in our family to go to college, she was doing great. She had never missed even one day of work so far—"

"Okay, okay," he said. "I'm getting the picture. Which reminds me, when you come in, bring a good picture. We'll get it on the air ASAP, provided she doesn't turn up before then. She could've just had car trouble, you know. Could be walking into town as we speak."

The officer's voice held no conviction. The fact that she apparently had a cell phone and didn't call to report a flat or other car trouble didn't bode well as far as the he was concerned. And that part about picking up a boy . . . that sounded like a bad joke. He would have to get a statement from the friend, but first, he was going to contact the Highway Patrol and get a duty report from the unit responsible for that stretch of highway. Maybe the trooper had seen something, an abandoned car, perhaps. "First things first," he muttered to himself, "that's what my mama always said. First things first."

***

Beth was so glad to finally be at the cabin. It brought back so many great memories, especially the memory of John, a huge young bear of a man. He had been wandering close to their cabin when her dad had spied him and called him over. His hair was dark blond hair and his eyes were the color of seawater.

Thinking of those eyes now made her recall the protective way he would "spot" her every time she was about to do something daring, like swinging from the ancient knotted rope out over the lake. She hadn't even known it was there, but when he showed it to her, she'd clambered up onto the giant boulder to reach it before he could test it first.

Remembering the way he'd stood, arms crossed over his bare chest, waiting for her to let go or return to the bank—poised to leap in and pull her out if necessary—those were the memories that had brought her back each and every year until she'd met and married Sam.

Beth rubbed her arms and put away the past. John had been eighteen and she barely fourteen. He had been like a big brother to her, gentle but annoying. They had fished with her dad and camped out in the woods. They'd built shelters and climbed mountains, all things tomboy that

Beth had loved back then. It had been absolutely . . . magical. And then he had simply disappeared. He'd never known how her feelings for him had changed over the course of that summer. They'd gone from platonic to knight-in-shining-armor crushy, and she had never told him.

The next trip to Stutter Creek, a few months later, she had cajoled her dad into taking her all the way up the mountain to John's cabin, but it had been deserted. He obviously hadn't been there in a long time. She never saw him again. He had told her he had an aunt in Houston, but his parents had died in a car crash when he was seven. He'd never mentioned his aunt's name; all Beth knew was that her last name wasn't the same as his.

When John finally did return to the mountain, he had immediately checked out the old Brannock cabin, but of course, it was empty. He supposed he should have been more forthcoming about his childhood way back when; how his aunt had taken him in after his parents death. And, also, how he'd always felt it was somehow his fault that she was so distant and disinterested. It wasn't that his aunt was cruel; she'd just been a career woman who didn't want children. Maybe if he had told Beth all that, then she would have understood why he had never returned to his little cabin near Stutter Creek. Even though he'd bought the property with his parents' insurance money, and even though he'd built his little cabin right in the middle of it, once he'd met Beth, his desire to live alone and hide from the world had disappeared. And yet, he never felt that he could admit that fact to anyone.

That was when he'd decided he needed to see some more of the world before he let himself become a hermit.

Years later, he finally admitted to himself that he had "lit out for the territories" mostly because he felt guilty as hell for having fallen for a fourteen-year-old girl.

He had set out to find a girl his own age. Someone with whom he might share the same sort of connection as the one he'd felt with Beth. In his journal, he's admitted that he was afraid something wrong with him. Why else would he have enjoyed such platonic, tomboyish things with a little girl and her dad? He had never enjoyed himself or felt so at ease in his whole life as the summer he spent with them at Stutter Creek.

Later, after he'd joined the Army and seen life behind enemy lines, he'd come to believe that it wasn't just Beth that had made him feel so different; it was Beth and being part of her relationship with her dad. He'd never realized how much he had missed out on when his own parents passed away. Eventually, John convinced himself that his feelings for Beth had just been brotherly, and he'd squashed down and ignored the fact that from then on he compared every girl he met to her.

***

Locking the car after her last trip with the ice chest, Beth stopped and listened to the forest. She'd always felt very lucky to have the National Forest as their back yard. It literally backed right up to their land. There would never be a subdivision or a dividing of their acreage. Her dad had lucked out when he'd bought the little five-acre plot so many years earlier.

Over the years she would intermittently talk her dad into hiking up to John's old cabin again, but he was never there. It just became more and more decrepit, as if the forest was in a battle to reclaim it, and the forest was winning.

Inhaling deeply, Beth savored the tang of pine. The humid air was like a balm. Her dad had loved these piney woods, the fragrance, the wildlife, the isolation, and especially the little creek that bordered the property. In fact, it was this very creek, the crystal clear Stutter Creek, which gave the small nearby town its name.

All her life, when they needed to get away, one or the other of them would utter the simple question, "Stutter Creek?" And in no time at all they would be packed and in the car. Eventually, she'd even mastered the art of "cabin" packing: pajamas, pair of jeans, couple tee shirts, cut-offs for swimming in the creek, bug spray, and some food. No makeup, hair dryer, curling irons, none of that. Just real life stuff.

Her daughter, Abby, had been the same way. She'd thought Sam was, too. Now, she just didn't know. Their whole life together seemed like little more than a sham. It was hard to even think about him anymore. It seemed like no matter which memory surfaced, she had to stop and examine it, to see if it had been tainted by the lie that was his infidelity.

In other words, he had burst her bubble, big time. No longer was she the Cinderella who had married her prince and lived happily ever after. Now she felt more like the village idiot; one who had never known everyone else was making fun of her all along. It seemed as if everyone had known about the affair but her.

All at once, standing in the driveway of her beloved cabin, Beth felt uncomfortable and exposed. She recalled the very thing that she had been trying to avoid thinking about—the boy. Or rather—the vision of the boy. She pushed away a maddening strand of hair. The night air was getting colder by the second. Her sweater was suddenly not enough. She rubbed her upper arms, trying to rub away the chill. Was someone watching her?

Turning a slow circle, Beth scanned the close tree line. She let her mind see, the way her father had taught her, vision widening, almost blurred, able to see the whole picture at once. Gestalt, her dad called it. See gestalt. And so she did. But there was nothing there that shouldn't have been. She was just getting herself worked up.

Once again, she turned toward the cabin. It was a small log structure, two rooms and a bath. The back room was just large enough for two double beds and a tiny, built on bathroom that beat the heck out of the outhouse they used the first few years. The square of light from the picture window at the front of the house fell upon the scant snow like thin buttermilk.

She stepped onto the porch just as a shadow crossed the window. For a split second, the snow reflected a dark shape moving across the light.

Beth hesitated, hand on the old-fashioned knob. It's just an insect, she thought, a large moth flying against the light fixture. It has nothing to do with the shadow-dream. Nothing! She exhaled, turned the knob and stepped inside. The cabin felt cozy. She could almost smell her father's after-shave, the scent of wood smoke that always reminded her of him.

If only he were here . . .

She quickly unpacked her jeans and shirts. She'd added a couple of sweatshirts and flannel shirts due to the season, and of course the required T-shirts, and she folded them all into the deep drawers of the chest between the beds. Socks and underwear went into the upper drawer, and her jacket she hung on a peg driven into the wall.

All done, she collapsed into the recliner in the living room/kitchen combination. The smell of her father was beginning to overwhelm her. His aftershave, the spicy aroma he'd worn year round, and the real smoky scent from the fireplace were surrounding her. She began to blubber, and this time the tears would not be stopped; they flowed freely, almost silently. She wiped them away on the sleeve of her shirt as she stared into the lovely, crackling fire. When she was finally done, she felt lighter, cleansed, almost hollow again.

Leaning back, Beth put her feet up and told herself she should fix something to eat. And so thinking, she drifted off to sleep, the rough corduroy fabric of the old recliner pressing trenches into the side of her face.

Outside the small cabin, a gentle breeze licked at the fresh snow, the moonlight illuminating the footprints of the fox in the driveway, and the footprints of a man near the creek.

Chapter Nine

"I can't just sit here, waiting," Kami told her mother. "I'm going to pick up Corey and we are going to drive every inch of Mandy's route from her dorm to her work."

Barb nodded, her eyes shimmering with unshed tears. "Do you have your cell phone?" she asked hesitantly.

Kami smiled and held it up. "Don't worry. I'll call as soon as we find her." Her voice cracked and she leaned over and hugged her mother tightly. "I'm calling Aunt Jean to come over and be with you while I'm gone."

Her mother started to interrupt, but Kami held up her index finger. "No, don't argue. It's a done deal. If Dad were still alive, I wouldn't bother. But he's not." She hurried out the door, already pressing numbers on her keypad. Over her shoulder she called, "And don't forget to lock your door!"

Sixty-five miles away, in Yellow Bend, a tiny suburb of Pine River, Officer Frank Lujan was about to make a discovery that would have him questioning his decision to become a police officer instead of a firefighter like he had once intended.

He'd only been a solo patrol officer for a couple of months, so when he saw an animal run across the street dragging something that looked like a human arm, he pulled the cruiser to the side of the road, slammed the gearshift into Park, and jumped out to give chase. It was only after the coyote dropped the arm that Officer Lujan realized it really *was* human.

"I thought it was part of a store dummy," he kept repeating when his backup arrived. "You know, one of those mannequin things. I didn't seriously think it was . . . real."

He couldn't say anymore. He was too busy attempting to regain his composure and figure out what to write on his report. Meanwhile, his backup had arrived and was on the radio calling for the Medical Examiner. After he signed off, he asked, "Which way did the coyote come from?"

Officer Lujan pointed to the east. "I guess I should start searching in that field."

The experienced officer shook his head. "First we'll cordon off the area. Then we'll wait for further instructions." He adjusted his utility belt. "Sarge might even want us to wait until daylight. Be less likely to trample evidence if we can see it."

The rookie understood the logic of waiting. But it really tested his patience to stand by, knowing that animals might be chewing on the remains of a human out there somewhere. He was very relieved when the Chief herself came down and told them a cadaver dog and its handler were being brought in as soon as possible.

Lujan and another officer stood watch the rest of the night, and when day broke, the dog was brought out. Within four hours it had pinpointed the rest of the young woman's remains. Dental records would be required to identify her. All they could tell for certain was that she had been a blonde female. There were traces of blonde hair still attached to her skull, and the Medical Examiner said the pelvis was definitely that of a woman.

***

Beth was groggy and disoriented when she awoke around three a.m.. For a moment, she had the idea she had run off the road and was stuck in a ditch. She expected the strange little boy to show up at any moment, but then the moonlight through the picture window reminded her where she was. The light was still blazing from the overhead fixture as well, because she had never gotten any further than the recliner. The fire was also still going, but now it was smoldering, glowing instead of crackling brightly.

After everything she'd been through, plus her experience beside the road, Beth was completely wiped out. She couldn't even remember the last time she'd eaten. As if on cue, her stomach rumbled loudly. Nothing like a little mental and emotional turmoil to work up an appetite.

She pressed a hand to her middle and wandered to the fridge while mentally cataloging the interior, which she had so recently filled. She rubbed her eyes again. Tiny lights flickered at the edge of her vision. Tired, she thought, rubbing gently. Too much driving and crying. Ought to write a country song. She laughed morosely. The lights flickered again, briefly. She switched on the single bulb over the sink, turned off the higher watt fixture over the table. Too much glare, maybe? Colored sparks jumped away into the air just outside her normal field of vision. If she tried to actually see them, they were gone. If she went gestalt, they were there: bright darts of light like a rainbow of electrical sparks.

"Damn," she turned on the tap to splash water on her face. "Hope I'm not getting a migraine." She'd had migraines when she was younger, none for years though. But with the stress she'd been under, anything was possible.

The water was cold. It woke her even more, but the flashes of light were still there. She shook her head. Maybe some food will help. She spread butter on bread for pan-fried toast.

"Couple slices of toast with peanut butter, maybe a dab of grape jelly, nothing like a little comfort food." Her voice in the empty cabin was quite loud.

Beth sighed. She still wasn't used to being alone.

The tiny kitchen was just big enough for one person. She moved from fridge to stove with ease. Her dad had always let her help in the kitchen, even when she had been too small to reach things, he would sit her on the counter and hand her whatever needed to be stirred or peeled or opened or poured. She remembered very clearly the first time he let her chop vegetables . . . she'd felt so grown up. Abby had been the same way. She loved to help in the kitchen and sit on the counter. She especially loved helping her Grampa. They were so close.

Why are we always in such a hurry to grow up and leave, Beth wondered? She sat at the small pine table and pondered that question. It had been on her mind a lot lately. But of course it would; she was missing both her dad and her daughter. And her once-best-friend, Sam. But I won't think of him. I just won't!

The toast turned to sawdust in her mouth and the memories crowded around like crows on a highline wire. Just the thought of how Sam had been when they were first married was enough to bring on the tears.

Oh what fun they'd once had, hiking, camping, exploring, and traveling. Loving. It had been an endless summer vacation. Try as she might, Beth couldn't really see where they'd gone wrong.

Heart heavy, she pushed away the once-good memories and poured herself a glass of milk. The toast she scraped into the garbage can. Now that she had let the memories in, they were rushing about her head just like the darting lights had done a few minutes earlier. "Sam, Sam, Sam," she whispered, angrily swiping at the tears that kept leaking.

"Why? I thought we had such a good thing. Twenty years . . . how can anyone just throw it all away? It would be easier if you'd died, like Dad. At least then my good memories would still be good—not tainted."

She sat back down in the recliner and let the memories flow: playing catch with an old baseball in the backyard when they were in their twenties, her wedding ring flying through the air because she'd gotten so thin from, according to her dad, living on love.

How amazed she had been when her new husband had taken an old costume ring and tossed it from the same place she had tossed the baseball, and how the cheap ring had landed deep in the thick grass within a few inches of her own precious wedding ring. The one she couldn't even look at now. The one that was locked up in her new safety deposit box back home, along with the twenty thousand in cash that her dad had left just for her in a thick envelope inside his old sleeping bag. Just in case you need some mad money, the note had read in his strong block print. That was what he always said when she was a teen and had first started going out with groups or on dates.

"Love you," he would say. Then he would press a ten or twenty into her palm and whisper, "Just in case you need some mad money."

She'd found out the hard way what he meant when she was barely sixteen and a school party had almost turned into her undoing. Rather than ride home with Cindy, her old friend and the girl who'd brought her, Beth had stupidly accepted a ride from a senior boy who just naturally assumed that since she was smitten with him, she was going to put out a little for his effort.

Fortunately, they hadn't gone far when she figured it out by the way his hand kept straying to her thigh. She had jumped out at the first red light, headed for the nearest convenience store, called a cab, and used the mad money to pay for it. And she never told her dad. She was so ashamed that she had done exactly what he'd always told her not to do. She'd gotten into a car with a boy she didn't really know.

But she had learned her lesson, and she never had to use the mad money again. When she was seventeen, she took all the unused money she'd been saving and bought her dad a new car stereo since his old one only played tapes, not CDs.

That was all so long ago. Now we've got satellite radio and iPods. And he is gone, too. Obsolete.

Beth shivered, either from the cold, or from the cold loneliness that had crept in again. When Sam left, she'd been in a total state of shock, then her dad died and all her friends and relatives came in an took over. They made all the arrangements, and they stayed with her and kept her from going insane. They also took care of Abby. Of course, her new son-in-law, Terry, had helped tremendously. But eventually they had all gone on with their lives. Just as they should have.

Now, she was truly alone. It was time, because if someone else had continued making all the decisions, then Beth might never get back on track. Cindy had been prepared to move in and stick around for "as long as it takes." But Beth had finally grown a backbone and sent her home, too. In the long run, it was for the best. Both Cindy and Abby were just a phone call away if she needed them.

She wondered aloud if her life would have turned out differently with someone else—John, for instance. She shook her head, scolding herself for such silly thoughts. We were little more than children. But the memory of his clear green eyes and strong, tanned arms warmed her. At least for the moment.

Chapter Ten

Kurt was getting antsy. He'd bought the Styrofoam ice chest and pup tent at Wal-Mart in Pine River a week after he'd snatched Danny from Albuquerque. Kurt loved Wal-Mart—so big and anonymous. The very place to find everything he needed. He'd known he would need a hiding place once he started implementing his plan. Cops start getting very suspicious when young women go missing.

He'd stashed the tent and supplies in the forest so he and Danny could go to ground when needed. He thought he knew where the cave was from the map he'd printed off Dave's computer. Actually finding it was another matter. Amanda Myer's cell phone probably had GPS. But cell phones were traceable. Anyone who watched cop shows on TV knew that was a sure fire way to get caught. He and Danny would just have to search using the new compass he'd bought. The cave was going to be his safe haven.

He was sitting on top of a boulder near a little creek as he surveyed the scene. The gurgling of the water calmed him. He wanted to make it the soundtrack for the demise of his next victim. Too bad he was going to lure her to his car using Danny as bait, just like he'd done with the other two.

Kurt had stopped to rest for a moment in his trek up the mountain. It was hard going, with the kid. He was constantly forced to stop and wait on him, or prod him into moving faster. At this rate, they might not locate the cave until tomorrow.

Kurt looked at the thick blanket of dead leaves on the ground. He decided to go ahead and pitch the tent here and spend the night beside the creek. Tomorrow, he would dope the kid up good, and then go in search of the cave on his own. There'd be no fire, though.

From one of the many pockets on his jacket, he pulled out a couple of packets of beef jerky and handed one to Danny. "We're stopping here," he said. Then he popped up the tent and allowed Danny to go inside to sleep. He didn't like having the boy out in the open. Even in the National Forest, there could be prying eyes. He had camouflaged the car with branches, but he knew from experience that one could never be too careful. The best thing to do would be to find that cave as quickly as possible. Then he could finish his business and get on with his life. He was beginning to crave getting high again.

As the sun slipped behind the mountain, Kurt sat on the boulder and reminisced. His first victim had been only a few days after he'd snatched Danny. He'd had to train Danny first, and then the rest had been easy.

Her name was Sherylyn Combs. She was a night clerk at the Wal-Mart in Pine River. Three days earlier he'd followed her to her car, an older model SUV. She must've been really tired. She never looked at him once. Didn't notice him at all. She lived in a rundown duplex in the suburb of Yellow Bend a few miles away. He had followed her again the next night, just to be certain she always took the same route.

Kurt had been driving the rusted Ford that he had obtained as part of a trade with Dave, the cokehead. Now, Dave was undoubtedly zoned out on his own urine stained sofa back in the big city, a tribute to the excellent Mexican brown heroin Kurt had turned him on to. Something he'd procured just for that purpose. At first, Dave had resisted, saying he was just a cocaine man. But when Kurt had turned to go, muttering about how he had plenty of other buddies who would want it, Dave had undergone a sudden change of heart.

Kurt had been so excited he couldn't wait to get started with his plan. He'd found Sherylyn on Facebook. She had listed Wal-Mart under "Where worked" on her profile page.

Kurt thanked Fate that all his camping supplies could be found at the same store where the first name on his list was a cashier. As soon as he entered, he picked her out of the line of cashiers. Her profile picture had obviously been taken a few pounds ago, but when he saw her face in profile, he was certain she was the one.

Whistling a lullaby under his breath, Kurt had unhurriedly gathered his supplies—Danny was passed out in the car under a blanket—and then he headed for Sherylyn's checkout stand. Her plastic nametag confirmed that she was definitely the one he wanted.

She'd made small talk as she scanned his ice chest, tent, and flashlight. "Going camping, huh?" She hadn't really looked at his face. Her hands moved with their own kind of grace and symmetry as they picked up each item, rolled it to find the bar code, then slid it effortlessly across the scanner. Beep.

Kurt had grinned and fingered the duct tape in his pocket. "Yep. Hunting, too." His voice was jolly. If Sherylyn had looked into his eyes, her hand motions would have been halted at the discrepancy between his jolly voice and the intent in his eyes.

But she hadn't looked up. Nor had she noticed the excitement coating his words. If she noticed anything at all, she never let on.

Kurt had felt a stirring his groin as he stood there talking to the first name on his victim list. In his mind, he was imagining her face contorted in pain.

Unaware of his excitement, Sherylyn had continued to scan the smaller items—beef jerky, Pepsi, bottled water—and then she sacked them up.

He paid with cash. No paper trail for Kurt Graham.

He was too smart for that.

Now, sitting on his boulder on the slope of the mountain, Kurt had become so lost in his gruesome thoughts that he almost missed the wedge of blue that flashed between the trees a hundred yards away. He'd known there was a cabin down there; he'd even briefly considered using it as his hideout, but it was way too close to the road. But what was that flash of blue? Was it a car?

He stood up on the boulder for a better look. The sun was almost down; it was difficult to see. No way. It couldn't be . . .

It was.

He jumped lightly from the boulder and followed the path of the creek for several minutes until he had a clearer view of the cabin.

A blue '69 Camaro sat in the circle driveway. He was close enough to hear the tick of the cooling engine.

Kurt grinned.

Fate had just smiled on him, again.

He was so high on his own morbid thoughts he never even noticed the large paw prints, in the soft Earth, that led from the creek toward the cabin.

Chapter Eleven

Even though she'd barely nibbled it, the toast and milk helped. Putting away the food and washing the skillet gave her mind something to focus on. Soon, Beth was able to blow her nose and put the sniffles away, too.

"Bedtime," she said to no one as she turned off the lights and went in search of the trashy gossip magazines Cindy had given her.

"Might help you get your mind off things," Cindy had said, stuffing the sack full of magazines into Beth's hands just before she left. "You really should get yourself a laptop computer—"

"I know," Beth agreed. "But there's no Internet at the cabin anyway." She had accepted the sack of magazines gratefully. Then she'd added the legal tablet Dalton had suggested she take. He thought writing her feelings down might help alleviate the nightmares.

That made perfect sense to Beth. She'd been taking notes in a spiral notebook for years. She wanted to write a novel. Having come from such a small family, she had always wanted to write a sprawling family epic. Something completely opposite of her real life. So she'd added that notebook to the pile of reading/writing material.

At least I don't have to be ashamed of my writing dreams anymore. Sam had always thought it was such a waste of time. Probably one reason I never took it very seriously myself.

After washing her face, brushing her teeth, and banking the fire one last time, Beth slipped into her sleep shirt, grabbed the pile of magazines, and proceeded to catch up on the latest doings of Hollywood's finest. She conked out so quickly she didn't even turn off the reading light.

About an hour later, the dreams began. She dreamed her father was standing beside the bed, waiting for her to wake up so they could go hiking.

"Where we going, Dad?" her dream-self asked.

Her father just smiled.

When she awoke, tiny flashes of colored light were popping merrily around her face. "Dad?" she asked, still caught up in the dream web. "S'that you?"

She thought she saw movement near the tall windows. "Dad?" Her voice was a bare whisper. "If that's you, this isn't funny . . . "

The spicy, smoky smell was heavy.

The reading light was still on. Beth sat up carefully, tired of being awakened every night. Outside the window opposite her bed, a faint shadow shifted.

"Who's there?" Her voice was a bit louder. The shadow grew still. I'm losing my mind, she thought. *I must be losing my mind. First the dreams, and the shadow, then the boy, and now more shadows, dear God!* She leapt from her bed and flipped on the overhead light.

All shadows were banished except for the one she herself was projecting. She waved at it to make sure it really was hers. And that's when she heard something running across the long wraparound porch.

Beth rushed to the window, but whatever it was had already made it to the woods. She could hear the sounds it made crashing through the underbrush. It sounded large and fast. This time, she was sure she had heard claws on wood. *Raccoon, perhaps. A BIG one.* She recalled that they sometimes got up to twenty or twenty-five pounds. *Certainly no shadow, that's for sure.*

Could it have been a small bear, a cub? They were pretty fast. At least she was sure it was some kind of animal this time. That meant she wasn't going crazy, she wasn't just imagining things. *Thank God! Just an animal. Not another formless dream-shadow.* Her breath eased and her heart slowed to normal.

I'll check for tracks in the morning. She was used to animals in the forest. In earlier years, they had sometimes seen bear tracks in the snow. But that had been many, many years earlier. The last time they had checked, when Abby was still at home, the park rangers said the bears had been gone from these parts for over a decade.

Still, it was comforting to know it was just an animal and not a malevolent dream-spirit or something equally bizarre. She wondered briefly about a human causing the noise; a peeping tom or such—but that was such an unlikely possibility that she shoved the thought away almost as quickly as it had occurred.

She checked the locks on all the doors and windows, as if that would keep out a malevolent shadow-spirit, and then she made the conscious choice to leave all the lights blazing thinking, *hoping,* that the light would deter anything from returning. Then she tried to go back to sleep.

This time, however, she took her pillow and blanket and curled up in the big recliner again. She got up one last time, dug her cell phone out of her purse, and plugged it into the charger she'd unpacked earlier. *Just in case I get a signal,* she thought.

Anything's possible.

***

Kurt stood close by the cabin, his filthy clothes helping him to blend in with the scenery even better than he could have planned. He couldn't believe his luck. It had to be the woman from the highway. *Luck? No, Fate.* They'd both been headed to the same place. On the other hand, the road they'd both been travelling led to the National Forest and not much else. He liked the idea of Fate better than luck. It meant he was supposed to take her.

As he checked his pockets to make sure he had his duct tape, he came across Amanda Myers' driver's license. A small chuckle escaped him and he pressed it to his lips before tucking it into a different pocket of his thrift-store jacket.

Sherylyn's Wal-Mart nametag inhabited the same pocket. His intention was to fill that zippered pocket with something from every girl on his list. Now, he would get to add something from one fate-kissed middle-aged woman who just happened to drive a very recognizable blue Camaro. Kurt chuckled again. This was turning out to be even better than he'd expected.

He leaned against a tree and pulled strips of beef jerky out of their plastic packet. Every now and then he caught a glimpse of the old broad roaming around inside the cabin. She was definitely still alone.

This was going to be fun.

Silently, he traipsed back up the mountain toward the tent where Danny lay, nearly comatose; his unopened packet of jerky still clutched in his filthy little hand.

Once again, Kurt wished he'd kept the cell phone he'd taken from Amanda Myers. He had thought about keeping it for a souvenir, but it had taken up too much room in his pocket. Besides, he was afraid it was traceable, even without the battery. He'd taken that out and tossed it beside the highway somewhere outside Pine River.

He still thought about the phone, though. That little green shell had appealed to him. It was so sparkly, a sweet reminder of the lovely girl herself. But at last, he'd decided to get rid of the shell, too. Just yesterday, he had buried it at the base of a tree like a tiny treasure. If he hadn't buried it, the green rhinestone cover would have been very vibrant against the thin layer of snow still on the ground.

***

Sunlight warming her face woke her. It was full daylight and she had actually slept undisturbed. Beth stretched and tried to stand. Her back was in kinks and her neck was so stiff it popped when she straightened it. I'll pay for sleeping in that chair, she thought, heading toward the shower.

The light on her phone had changed from red to green so she plucked it from the charger as she walked by. No calls, the screen said, but she flipped to the address book and started to scroll down the list. She thought she should at least try to call Cindy and let her know she had made it to the cabin. With her thumb, she sent the cursor flying down the list. It scrolled past Cindy and stopped on Dad.

She started over. The same thing happened. She couldn't get it to stop on Cindy. It would just go straight to Dad. She tried to land the cursor on Abby's phone number. Same thing happened. It went straight to Dad.

Beth was getting angry. "Now my phone's going to fall apart," she declared pessimistically. She pushed the scroll-down arrow and held her thumb on it. The little cursor flew up and down the list of contacts over and over again until she finally took her thumb away. It landed squarely on Dad, again.

She gave up, touched OFF, and vowed to try again after her shower. *Guess I should take his number out of my contact list.* She shoved that idea aside and thought; maybe it will help if I just take the phone outside. But deep down she knew that wouldn't make a difference like it sometimes did with signal reception. Getting a signal had nothing to do with numbers already stored in her contact list.

Sighing, she turned on the shower and let it warm up while she brushed the knots from her hair. Hope the water works as well on my knotted muscles, she thought.

She unwrapped a new bar of Dove bath soap, unpacked her shampoo and conditioner, and then went in search of towels and washcloths.

As usual, her dad had left them, neatly folded, in the skinny metal cabinet they'd installed beside the shower so many years earlier. Like the bed linens, everything was folded and tucked inside spare pillowcases, which were easier to wash and kept their contents fresh and dust free.

At last she stepped into the shower. The warm water was amazing. She could feel the kinks and knots loosening up in her neck and spine. Soaping away all of yesterday's grime and depression, she immediately began to feel better, calmer, more like herself than she had in quite a while. "Knew I would feel better at Stutter Creek," she murmured, rinsing.

Wrapping a towel around her hair, and another around her body, Beth began to hum a meaningless tune. She dressed quickly and combed her shoulder length hair. For once, she didn't mind the tiny streaks of gray showing through her bangs. She hadn't thought about getting it colored to cover them like she usually did; she hadn't had time to think about a lot of things lately.

Oh well, she decided, I only kept it colored for Sam anyway. Might as well begin to act my age, got no one to impress anymore. Not that coloring it had done any good. He'd left her for someone barely out of her twenties. She gritted her teeth and fought away the ridiculous tears.

"I will not shed another tear on that worthless excuse of a man," she scolded herself. "He can't throw me away, he's the trash not me." By now she was whispering, trying to bolster her own flagging self-image and fight off the tears at the same time. Gazing into the medicine cabinet mirror, her eyes appeared almost blank, so tired and empty. Her good feeling was slipping away—

A tiny beep interrupted her thoughts. She glanced at the phone suspiciously.

A signal, now? Who could be calling? Oh, probably Cindy. I'll bet she's worried sick because I haven't checked in.

Apology on her lips, she picked up the phone. But it wasn't an incoming call. It was a text. Now why didn't I think of that, she wondered. Sometimes a text will go through when a call won't.

THAT'S MY GIRL, the text read.

Beth stared at the message.

The info line read: Dad. There was no accompanying number.

She laid the phone down and stepped away from it as if it had suddenly grown fangs. The room swayed; colored lights darted about her face, visible only in her periphery. She felt her consciousness trying to slip away, then remembered her first aid training from school: head between knees, head between knees, head be—

She slid down to the floor and hung her head between her knees, hands on the back of her neck. It worked. After a minute or two the grayness began to abate. Remembering to breathe helped, too.

She looked at the silent phone.

It beeped again and she picked it up gingerly.

YES, the new text said, *IT'S ME, DAD. AND YOU HAVE WASTED TOO MANY TEARS ON SAM ALREADY.*

Beth put the phone down again. She didn't *feel* like she'd lost her mind . . . could someone be playing a joke? Cindy? Abby? *Dalton?* They were the only ones who knew where she was. She thought and thought but couldn't come up with any reason not to believe. There was his smell, too. Beth knew she hadn't been imagining that. Finally, she picked up the phone. "Dad?" she texted.

YES, IT REALLY IS ME. SORRY I SCARED YOU.

Beth closed her eyes and chewed her bottom lip anxiously. *Anything's possible; men have walked on the moon, sent cameras into human bodies, transplanted entire faces and hands; but still, texting with the spirit of her father? How could it be?*

"I can't believe this," she said aloud as she texted. "Can we really communicate this way? How did you find out?" She opened her eyes to slits as if that would help her zero in on reality. Questions were popping up in her mind like bubbles in boiling water.

He replied: *I WAS WATCHING WHEN YOU WERE TRYING TO DECIDE WHETHER TO TAKE MY NAME OUT OF YOUR CELL PHONE.*

"So that's why it kept going to your name and no one else's?"

YES.

"Oh Dad, I can't believe you're still with me!" Tears coursed down her face, unheeded. "I wasn't going to take you out—never. But I couldn't stand the thought of dialing you by mistake. Just thinking about the phone ringing in that empty house made me so damn sad . . . "

WISH I COULD HUG YOU, he said.

Sobs burst forth like soda from a shaken can. "Me too," she sputtered.

DON'T KNOW HOW LONG I'LL BE HERE. HAVE TO MOVE ON SOON.

"What's it like, where you are?" Beth blurted. "Where *are* you, exactly?"

LOL, he wrote, *IT'S DIFFICULT TO SAY . . . I THINK I'M IN TRANSIT.*

"Heaven?" Beth had to ask.

SOON, he replied. *BUT YOU NEED ME NOW.*

"I do," she cried. "But I *always* will." All of a sudden, she realized she wasn't texting anymore, just speaking aloud. "I don't even have to type the letters, do I?"

NO, he texted. *I CAN HEAR YOU JUST FINE, BUT I HAVE TO TEXT. BE EASY ON YOURSELF. TIME REALLY DOES HEAL. I'M ALL RIGHT NOW AND WE'LL BE TOGETHER AGAIN SOMEDAY. SOON, I'LL SEE YOUR MOM. I CAN HARDLY WAIT. SHE WAS JUST A GIRL.*

Beth gave up. She couldn't respond to that. Thinking of her parents together after all this time made her so happy, and yet so extremely sad, it was like she had ridden a roller coaster right into the middle of a time warp.

TAKE CARE, he wrote. *I'LL BE AROUND.*

That reminded Beth of something. "Dad," she called to the seemingly empty room. "Are you still here?"

The phone beeped in her hand. *YES.*

"Can you, ya know, see me?"

YES.

"All the time?"

ONLY WHEN YOU REALLY, REALLY NEED ME. THAT MAKES ME . . . FOCUS.

Beth noticed the small flashes of light in her peripheral vision. "Is that you?"

YES, he replied.

Beth stopped and thought. "In the car, on the way here, were you with me?"

YES. YOU WERE VERY UPSET.

Nodding, Beth said, "I thought I sensed you." She hesitated, but had to ask. "Did you see a little boy?"

He sent back a row of question marks.

"Guess not," she said. "Can you see *any* other people?"

*NO. JUST YOU. BUT I FELT SOMETHING . . .
DARK. GLAD I CONVINCED YOU TO DRIVE ON.
BE CAREFUL!*

Beth flashed back to her decision to speed away from
the boy. "I'll be careful," she said. "I promise."

I'M NODDING, he wrote.

"By the way . . . when did you get so good at texting?
And how are you doing it?" Her voice was jovial. She
couldn't help it. She felt so much lighter now. So much
more *hopeful*. In the back of her mind, however, she was
recalling some of the stories from the grief group. *Could this
be a major hallucination like the woman who kept seeing her son every
night?*

NOT SURE WHY I CAN TEXT, he replied. *I JUST
THINK IT, AND THERE IT IS! ELECTRICAL
ENERGY, I SUPPOSE.*

Beth was quiet. All the films she'd seen about people
with mental illnesses began to flutter through her head as if
on an old-fashioned movie reel: *One Flew Over the Cuckoo's
Nest; Girl, Interrupted; Ordinary People; A Beautiful Mind.* Was it
possible she was so disconnected from reality that she
didn't even know it? First the shadows, then the little boy,
now this? Had she suffered a split from reality? *Had she?*

The phone beeped.

A question mark stood alone on the text line.

"Sorry, Dad," she said, still wondering if she was
actually talking to herself. "Electrical energy, huh? I guess
that's as good an explanation as any. But Dad, am I going
to lose you all over again?" She bit her lip, hating herself for
even asking, wondering if losing him again might, in fact,
herald her complete mental breakdown.

I WILL GO, he said. *BUT YOU WON'T BE SAD.
YOU WANT ME TO BE WITH MOM. I PROMISE I*

WON'T GO UNTIL THIS DARKNESS HAS PASSED. UNTIL YOU DON'T NEED ME ANYMORE.

Beth sighed. "You may wish you hadn't said that."

LOVE YOU, he wrote.

"You, too, Dad," she said. Then she added their old father-daughter mantra, "Always and forever." She started to touch OFF again, but thought of something else. "Just one more thing," she called.

YES?

"Why can you hear me talking, but I have to *see* your texts? Why can't we just converse, you know . . . somewhat normally?" She bit her lip, wondering if that question was the one that would unravel the fantasy and force her sick mind to realize she wasn't really talking to the spirit of her dead father.

I'M SORRY. I DON'T KNOW ALL THE ANSWERS. I JUST KNOW THAT I CAN HEAR, BUT I CAN'T SPEAK. MAYBE IT'S LIKE THE SKELETON SAID WHEN ASKED WHY HE DIDN'T GO TO THE PROM: I CAN'T GO, I DON'T HAVE NOBODY! LOL

Beth laughed at the old joke. Even in death, he still tried to keep things light. *Could it be real?* She pondered the situation for several minutes, her mind on autopilot.

"Love you," she whispered, just in case it wasn't a complete hallucination. Finally, she remembered she wanted to go out and check for tracks around the cabin.

The day had dawned cool and overcast. Spears of sunlight shot through the clouds here and there, illuminating the serene surroundings. *If there is a heaven,* she thought. *I hope it looks, and smells, just like this.*

She walked around the entire cabin. Sure enough, around back, beneath the tall, narrow, bedroom window, just off the wide porch, huge paw prints led straight up the mountain.

She followed the tracks with her eyes until they became invisible in the leafy ground cover. Might follow those later, she thought. *They don't look like bear tracks.* Definitely not raccoon. *Had wolves been reintroduced into the National Forest?* She couldn't remember reading about it if they had. That was only Alaska, maybe Montana . . . surely not New Mexico.

"Maybe I shouldn't follow them until I talk to someone in town. Have to be careful now that I'm on my own." She thought briefly of the conversation she'd had with her Dad on the cell phone.

Maybe I'm not completely alone after all. Could it be?

She wandered back inside to straighten up the kitchen.

Her mind was so preoccupied; she never saw the human tracks near the creek.

From the forest, a pair of amber eyes watched the cabin intently.

Chapter Twelve

Beth had cleaned every inch of the tiny cabin, and now she was holding her cell phone up in front of her face as she walked around the dappled perimeter of the clearing, hoping for a signal. She felt as if she were trying to contact the mother ship. In fact, she was trying to contact Cindy.

Finally, she gave up and started back inside with a sigh. *Have to drive down the mountain and see if that helps. Need to visit Stutter Creek anyway. See if the little drugstore is still there.*

All of a sudden, she remembered she was going to try texting. *Even if it doesn't go through right away, it might go through as soon as a signal is available.* At least that's the way she assumed it worked. *Only thing to do is try.*

She sent Cindy a quick note that said: *Arrived safely. No signal. Will try to call later.* She also sent the same message to Abby.

Taking even that small bit of action made her feel more connected. Now she could concentrate on other things.

As she walked back to the cabin, she heard a crashing sound coming from the trees.

Something was coming.

She cleared the porch in two leaps and dashed inside the cabin. She whirled about, slammed the heavy wooden door and grabbed the thick crossbar, sliding it across the doorway, jamming it home inside the square iron hook on each side. As far as she could remember, it was the first time the crossbar had ever been put to use except as a curiosity.

Suddenly, she was glad for the extra protection.

Standing rock-still in the middle of the cabin, breath coming in ragged gasps; Beth listened hard for the creature that was making all the noise. *Bear? Mountain lion? Wolf?*

Nothing. The woods were silent. She didn't hear even a bird; in fact, the only thing she could hear now was the pounding of her heart and the rasp of air in and out of her nostrils.

She swiped her hair away from her forehead wondering if she had just imagined how loud the sound had been. Then she remembered something else: "Dad," she whispered, "you still here?" She glanced down at the silent phone in her hand. When it beeped, she almost threw it against the wall.

STILL HERE, the message read.

Beth exhaled shakily. "Do you know if someone or some*thing* is near the cabin?"

Several seconds went by. Then a minute. Then two. Beth was about to speak again when the phone beeped.

THERE WAS MOVEMENT OF SOME KIND. GONE NOW.

She felt the flesh on the backs of her arms prickle at the thought of someone, or something, watching her. *Had someone had been staying in the cabin while it was empty?* It had never happened before, but she'd heard of it happening to others. Then she remembered the paw prints.

"I'm scared," she said. "I've never been scared here, not even as a child. Dad, you don't think it was a bear or a wolf, do you?"

NOTHING LIKE THAT. A DEER MAYBE. AM I SCARING YOU?

"No," she insisted. "Well, maybe at first, but not now. I just hope you'll be with me awhile. It doesn't even seem strange anymore. I guess I always knew there was more to this afterlife stuff than people let on . . ."

LOL

"Do you feel the same as when you were . . ."

ALIVE?

"Yes."

NOT AT ALL. NO PAIN, NO SORROW. NOW I JUST . . . AM.

Beth thought about that for a moment. She was so thankful he was out of pain. She felt the survivor's guilt begin to fade. Then she thought of something more: "Hey, how do you know if someone else was around the cabin—didn't you say you could only see me?"

YES, BUT CAN SEE A STREAK OF ENERGY IF SOMETHING'S MOVING.

"Oh," she replied. "I understand, I guess." She caught a tiny flash of light when she glanced up from the phone. "I see you," she said, and then she hesitated. "But I always thought spirits appeared as orbs or ghosts . . ."

THERE ARE SO MANY THINGS WE DIDN'T KNOW. I'M STILL LEARNING.

"I can't believe I'm talking to you!" Beth felt like a child who has just learned that people really can flap their arms and fly, like that Ray Bradbury story she'd once read.

ME EITHER. BUT WE ALWAYS HAD A SPECIAL CONNECTION. DO YOU REMEMBER GRAN'S "VISITS?"

Beth nodded. "She's been on my mind a lot lately."

I CAN'T WAIT TO SEE HER AND YOUR MOM. I'VE GOT TO MOVE ON SOON. MY ENERGY IS BECOMING . . . SCATTERED. HARDER TO FOCUS.

Beth felt the guilt rush back. "Of course, Dad, you go. I'm fine, really." And oddly enough, she was fine, or at least much better. Just knowing her father hadn't completely ceased to exist made her feel so much more hopeful. It was confirmation, just like he'd promised when she was a little girl.

***

John and Turk were taking their usual daily stroll, still getting used to the lay of the land, when Turk decided to dash on ahead. Something had piqued his interest. It looked as if he was headed toward the Brannock's old cabin. John let him run. He was certain no one was staying there.

But when he saw the vehicle in the driveway, he was shocked.

Guess I was wrong.

He stared at the cabin through the trees. From this distance, he couldn't tell much about it. He called Turk back to his side and proceeded to move in for a closer look.

It was around noon, the time most people went indoors to have lunch. He eased his way down to the edge of the clearing. The pine needles were thick beneath the massive trees. It made the going slippery; but that's why he wore lug-soled boots. Checking his field glasses—the small set that he always carried in one of the deep pockets of his camouflage jacket—John scanned the area around the cabin.

A classic Camaro was parked on the circle drive squarely in front of the cabin door. He could see a few footprints going to and from the car to the front door and back to the car again. Carrying in supplies, he thought. He could also discern places where the thick carpet of pine needles had been disturbed in a circular pattern. It appeared that someone, a woman by the size of the footprints, had stood and turned around and around in a circle. Doubt if she was dancing, John thought. *Wonder what made her do that?*

Though he had dealt with a few unsavory females in his line of work over the years, the majority of his contacts were men. John actually didn't have too much experience second-guessing women. He knew one thing for certain though; women and men *did* think differently. Or maybe that was just his opinion. Or his gut feeling. He depended on his gut *a lot*. Like now.

He'd been here for a couple of weeks, and besides wild life, the only other creatures he'd seen were the father and son campers who appeared to have stayed only the one night. Turk was sure acting differently, though. Maybe that was the reason his own hackles were standing at attention.

Then he saw them, the larger tracks encircling the cabin.

Even an amateur could tell that these were not the normal comings and goings of the inhabitants of the cabin; these tracks were furtive. They stopped beside nearly every window. Due to the damp soil, it was easy to see where the maker of the tracks even walked on tiptoe sometimes. Of course, some of the tracks weren't really footprints at all. They were more like smeary places in the pine needles; places were someone's foot had slid the ground cover aside as they jockeyed for position, probably for a better view.

Most of the snow was gone now, except for the deeply shaded places under the pines. Those dark pockets still held traces of white, and it was there that John was able to scout out even more prints.

But it was the ones near the windows that bothered him most. "All the better to see you said the big bad wolf," John muttered, stroking his beard thoughtfully. In his mind, he had a very good image of a peeping tom circling the small cabin, spying on the occupants as they moved around inside, thinking they were safe.

That image made his blood boil. This was just the sort of vermin he'd been paid to guard against over the years; people who preyed on others.

Times have sure changed, he thought. This is what I came here to get away from. He shook his head and backed carefully away from the cabin. It was impossible to be certain that the larger prints were from a predator. After all, the smaller prints in the front drive went around and around in circles, too.

It wasn't anything he could put his finger on, but he had suddenly developed a bad feeling. Not because someone was staying in the old Brannock cabin, but because the atmosphere of the forest had changed—as if he wasn't the only dangerous man in the woods anymore.

With a wave of his hand, John let Turk know it was safe to scour the perimeter. Another wave, just a finger actually, told Turk to backtrack a few paces to make sure no one had crossed their trail after they had come down the mountain. If he had scented anything unusual, Turk would have stopped and waited for further instructions.

As they completed their perimeter search, John stopped a few feet behind Turk. They both stared at the cabin. Turk's ears perked up. He could hear someone. .

John didn't know who might be in the cabin or how long they'd been there. He had no way of knowing if Tom still owned it or if he had sold it to someone else. He seriously doubted that the Brannock family still had possession of it. It would be ridiculous to even think that Beth could possibly still come here. By now she would be married with grown children.

Besides, when he and Turk had returned to the mountain, he'd checked her cabin even before he'd checked his own. It had appeared deserted, just like a seasonal vacation cabin would.

And if it *was* still theirs, truth be told, he didn't want to be introduced to Beth's husband and family. When he had known her, she was just a girl with her whole life ahead of her. He wasn't sure he wanted to see who had become a part of it. He didn't want to meet the man who had stolen her heart.

On the other hand, he wouldn't mind seeing her father, Tom Brannock. He thought maybe later he would ask around in town- try to determine if Tom was still around. But he didn't like involving others in his business, and he didn't like to appear nosy. Besides, running surveillance was second nature to Big John and Turk. He made a mental note to check back on the cabin tomorrow, and to let the local park ranger know about the footprints. Right now, though, he had more furniture to unload and a fridge to stock.

On the journey back up the mountain, he had to call Turk twice to come. The dog wanted to stay at the cabin. On impulse, John veered off the trail in order to check on the cold camp he'd stumbled across yesterday.

The man had looked like any other inexperienced camper. John had only caught a glimpse, and he didn't let himself be seen. He'd watched for a while, and then decided the scruffy young man was just a sometime camper with poor outdoor skills trying to spend some time with his kid. He was just setting up what had appeared to be a spanking new tent and ice chest. The kid had crawled inside the tent just as John had approached.

They were gone. John was glad. He figured the dad had filled his kiddy-time quota for the weekend. Probably only had the kid on the weekend; that's how most marriages seemed to work out these days. For a moment, John was glad he had never married; he didn't think he could ever be happy being a part-time Dad like that.

Maybe that's just my own background showing through. Always thought I'd give a kid the childhood I didn't get. Guess that'll never happen. Too damn old to start a family now.

He patted Turk's tawny coat and they tromped on through the woods. "Too bad you were off chasing squirrels yesterday," he said to the big dog. "I wonder what you would have made of that guy. I just really didn't like the looks of him, not even from a distance." To himself he muttered, "Gotta let go of the job. Constant paranoia isn't the way to live in the real world."

Chapter Thirteen

To pass the time at the camp, Kurt would pull out the items he'd taken off his two victims so he could amuse himself by reliving their last moments.

His first victim had been Sherylyn Combs, the Wal-Mart clerk.

The night had been calm, the moon in hiding. Underneath their feet, the shoulder of the road had been hard and unforgiving. Kurt liked that—no footprints. Within five minutes, Sherylyn's SUV came around the curve.

For a moment Kurt thought he'd overestimated how close the boy was standing. It looked like Sherylyn was going to mow him down and keep on going, but at the very last second, she had stomped on the brakes, skidded a bit, and then came to a shuddering stop just a few feet past their position.

Kurt was hidden in the bar ditch along with Dave's ratty old Ford.

Danny never blinked, but Kurt found that the whole near-miss thing had him so excited he'd folded the duct tape over on itself in the palm of his hand. He had to hurriedly yank a new length off the roll in his backpack. By then the SUV was slowly backing up to where Danny still stood, waiting.

That's when Kurt had struck, uncoiling himself from his hiding place without so much as a warning rattle. He'd actually crawled up behind Danny and yanked the boy out of the way by the cord tied around his waist, and then he'd simply leapt into the unlocked door of the SUV.

Being his first time to practice what he had previously only fantasized about, Kurt had even more trouble with the duct tape. The second piece he tore off the roll got tangled up in her hair. The third piece wouldn't stick the way it should have.

He freaked out, his breath like a furnace burning in his chest. Heaving, struggling, he held the woman down, yanked the second strip of tape from her hair, along with several huge clumps of blonde hair, and then he finally just wadded the whole mess into a spiky ball and crammed it into her mouth.

Sherylyn bit his fingers when he forced her lips apart. But it didn't bother him, he simply grasped her chin and shoved it closed with the heel of his hand. She clawed his face, his cheeks, his arms. She tried to get a grasp on the door handle—but Kurt had her smashed against the driver's door. He was snarling like a rabid beast.

Blood trickled from her scalp where he'd yanked the hair out, and now he had one wrist in his steel grasp, and the other arm was bent behind her, useless. Her legs were completely trapped beneath the steering wheel, his hard knee crushing her right thigh.

Kurt head-butted Sherylyn when she tried to grab the gearshift. Then he cranked up the volume on the radio and smiled when he heard the refrain of "Blue Eyes Crying in the Rain."

As Willie Nelson continued to wail, Sherylyn did her best to get rid of the wad of duct tape in her mouth, but Kurt went wild. He loosened his grip on her chin. Sherylyn whooped air through her suddenly open mouth just as Kurt thrust his entire hand between her teeth. Her jaw was forced open with a craaack, and he crushed the ball of tape down into her throat.

Completely panicked, Sherylyn whipped her head back and forth, but she could not dislodge the tape. His fist was iron.

The ball of tape slowly strangled Sherylyn.

Kurt's breathing quickened even more. His heart galloped in his chest.

The struggle, the blood, the unbridled fear and fight for survival—this was what he had longed for. Five years had been worth it after all.

He looked into her eyes, relishing the dimming of the light as her life ebbed away.

Kurt didn't want it to end, but he knew another vehicle could happen by at any second. Slowly, like a lover moving in for a first kiss, he covered her nose with his mouth, holding her nostrils closed with his teeth, cutting off her last hope of air.

Sherylyn briefly renewed her struggles.

But it didn't matter. All the little nips and scratches she'd managed to inflict were beautiful to Kurt.

After he sealed her nose, it was all over.

No air was getting past that ball of tape in her throat.

At last, he sat back, breathing heavily from exertion and excitement.

Sherylyn gave a huge gasp through her nostrils, clicked open the door with her now free hand, and tumbled out onto the ground.

For Kurt, the night became three-dimensional for the very first time. The chance that someone might happen along while his victim was crawling along the pavement like a wounded animal was a new kind of high, better than meth, even better than heroin. Nothing he'd ever tried could compare to this feeling of power. He felt reborn.

Perhaps the list is too short, he thought.

Maybe I've finally found my purpose in life.

He followed her out the open door and fell upon the poor girl as she tried to dig the tape out of her throat with both hands.

It took a lot longer for her to die than he'd anticipated. Her will to live was incredible. But in the end, his will was stronger. He'd simply smashed her face onto the pavement and sat on her, one knee on each outstretched arm. Unable to remove the tape or him on her back, Sherylyn had finally choked to death on the cold, hard ground.

Kurt hauled her back into the vehicle and shoved her limp body down into the front passenger side floorboard.

Then he retrieved a very groggy Danny from the Ford—he'd managed to crawl back inside after Kurt yanked him out of the way—and stashed him in the back of the SUV.

The drugged boy never uttered a word. He curled up in a ball and went to sleep immediately.

Leaving the Ford sheltered in the stand of trees, Kurt had then driven Sherylyn's SUV a few miles past the street where she lived. He'd scouted the area thoroughly the day before. He knew all about the abandoned gravel pit just outside the city limits of the sprawling suburb.

It was there that he finally gave in to the raging desire that had been building inside him since the moment the doomed girl had pulled over to check on Danny. He'd never wanted a warm body nearly as much as he wanted this cooling one. Maybe it was the fact that her name was so similar to his dead wife's. Or perhaps it was because he'd been stroking her blond hair the entire time he'd been driving.

When he stopped at the gravel pit, Kurt made certain Danny was still passed out before he went around to the passenger side and pulled his victim onto the front seat.

He didn't even mind that her face was all bruised and bloated from choking to death on the wad of tape. He unzipped his filthy jeans and shoved himself into Sherylyn's mouth. When he struck the spiky ball of tape still wedged in her throat, he groaned with pleasure. The pain was exquisite. Kurt shut his eyes and grimaced as the orgasm shook him. He thought he'd had sex before; he thought he'd climaxed, but even with the help of coke or meth there was no comparison. Spoiled, he thought, as the spasm subsided. Spoiled for sure, now.

He wished he had some place to store her; he really wanted to experiment. No time, though. He zipped his fly and kissed the dead girl on the forehead.

Then he dragged Sherylyn's body to the lip of the old pit and pushed her over. Afterward, he stripped a few branches off the nearest sage bush and tossed them down to cover her. He also used one of the branches to sweep away his tracks as he hurried back to the SUV. He'd seen that maneuver in an old western movie when he was a kid.

He felt so smart when he drove her SUV to the meanest section of town and made a show of locking it up tight. He knew it would be stripped before morning. No one would report it as abandoned. In fact, once they found that the keys were in the ignition, someone would have a high old time joyriding until the gas ran out. Or, if he was really lucky, a pro would find it and the pieces would be across the border before the sun rose.

It was quite a long walk back to the old Ford, but he couldn't risk leaving it there. His buddy, Dave, might sober up long enough to remember who had it.

On the way back to the Ford, when he wasn't pulling Danny by his "leash" or luring him along with a bottle of Pepsi like a carrot on a stick, Kurt went through Sherylyn's purse. First, he took the cash, just a few bucks, and then he took his first real treasure: her Wal-Mart nametag. He couldn't wait to start his collection and add to it. He kept his short list of five names in his pocket along with his "work" gloves.

He stuck the nametag in the same pocket. Later, he would separate them. He didn't want his treasures falling out the next time he needed his gloves.

The rest of her things he tossed into storm drains and dumpsters along the way. Kurt had been tempted to use the credit cards, especially the ATM card, but he'd watched too many crime movies while in prison. He knew ATM's had hidden cameras, and he knew credit cards left paper trails. He wasn't stupid.

The purse, itself, went into an empty field. Let the coyotes eat the leather, he thought. Then he began to enjoy the moonless walk. The air was fragrant with dark hope; he felt as if fate had smiled on him for the first time in his sorry life.

Even the things he hadn't planned had worked out in his favor—like the absence of a moon; like the fact that Sherylyn was off for the next two days. No one would raise an alarm for at least two days, maybe even three. By then, the animals and the elements would be well on the way to disguising her identity. Kurt began to hum Brahms Lullaby. His blonde girl was sleeping; with luck, she wouldn't be disturbed for quite some time.

The cool night air agreed with him. He actually surprised himself when he picked Danny up and carried him for a while after the boy had stumbled for the third or fourth time. Couldn't leave the kid behind in the open. That was the one thing they could definitely trace back to him. But he wasn't ready to get rid of him, yet. He was proving to be quite a nice accomplice.

He licked his lips, savoring the small cuts he felt there. Now he could begin to think about the second name on his list, Amanda Myers.

Chapter Fourteen

Beth couldn't sit still. After her "conversation" with her father, she had to get out and do something. She decided to drive into the tiny village of Stutter Creek and see if she could pick up a signal along the way. She really needed to talk to someone, preferably Cindy. She was also eager to check out the old drugstore. It was the one place they'd always visited on their trips to the cabin.

As she pulled on her jacket, she glanced out the window at her car. Better fill up with gas while I'm there, she thought. She grabbed her purse and locked the door securely as she went out.

She was rubbing the old skeleton key, thinking of all the things her dad had said, when out of nowhere she heard the sound of an animal crashing through the brush again.

Just like a scream-queen in a horror movie, Beth accidentally dropped the keys in the dirt before she could get the car door open. So she turned and ran. She wasn't sure where she was going, but in the back of her mind was the irrational thought that she'd be safer off the ground, up a tree.

She didn't make it.

The animal was upon her before she'd gotten completely turned around.

"Hey!" she yelled, when she realized it was a dog and not a bear. "Get off me you big bully!"

She couldn't believe the huge mutt actually had her forearm in his jaws.

But Beth didn't have time to register fear. The situation was just too ridiculous.

"I said, let go!" She yanked her arm free of the loose grip of the huge jaws. Her jacket sleeve was gummy with slobber.

"Yuck!" She shook her arm to get rid of the drool. "That was totally uncalled for."

At last, Beth realized how tremendously huge the dog was. When he sat down at her feet, his head came up to her chest. If he had stood on his hind legs, he would have dwarfed her.

Now that the adrenalin rush was over, and she realized how easily he could have really hurt her, Beth's bones turned to mush and she actually put her arm across the dog's shoulders for support.

"You scared me half to death," she said. "Where's your owner?" She tried to read the tag on the woven collar, but the dog wouldn't allow it. He shook his head comically every time she grasped it.

"What?" she asked. "Are you travelling 'indognito' or something?"

Another wag of the tail convinced her she was right. But she was so taken by his doggy grin that she cautiously walked back to her car, retrieved her keys, which he seemed very curious about, and went back inside the cabin for a doggy bribe.

Beth was not surprised when the dog accompanied her to the door and stopped. However, she also wouldn't have been surprised if he had followed her inside and made himself at home. He acted as if he belonged there.

All she could find in the way of doggy treats was an unopened package of Oscar Meyer Wieners.

He liked them just fine; in fact, she quickly discovered that he would do almost anything for a hot dog. By the third one, he was on his back and she was rubbing his belly.

She wondered what had caused the mass of scar tissue on his shoulder, but he didn't seem too sensitive about it.

After the fourth hot dog, there was no turning back. She tried to read his tag again, but he still twisted away when she touched his collar. Beth thought it wise not to push her luck.

For just a second, she wondered if the dog could possibly have anything to do with the spirit of her father. She'd always been intrigued by the idea of reincarnation, but after a few minutes, she knew it couldn't be true. This dog was so goofy he would definitely have been a comedian in another life. On the other hand, her father did love to goof around. Nah, she thought. That's even more ridiculous than the texting.

Finally, after the sixth hot dog, the big mutt suddenly shot to his feet, ears at attention, and cocked his head to one side as though he needed to concentrate on a sound. Then, before she could even react, he was gone. He'd cleared the porch, the steps, and the circle drive in three leaps.

"Hey," she called after him. "It's not nice to eat and run!"

She went back inside, washed her hands, and decided to go on into town. At least now I know what made the gosh-awful racket crashing through the woods and running around on the porch. Better get some dog biscuits, though, she thought, smiling. Hot dogs might get expensive. She was pretty sure she'd see the big galoof again. At least she certainly hoped so.

She didn't see the dog anywhere when she pulled out of the drive, but she was certain he lived nearby. If he had been a stray, his coat would have been matted and he would've eaten ALL the hotdogs whether she offered them, or not.

There were no more distractions. Beth actually began to feel relieved, happy almost. She'd read more than one article that said dogs are good for the soul. They can supposedly help alleviate depression and anxiety, too. In the back of her mind, she was reiterating her earlier thoughts about visiting the Sandy Animal Shelter. Lots of animals need homes. If one didn't find her when she got back, as they usually seemed to do, then she would just have to search them out on her own. It gave her something to look forward to. It had been quite a while since she had lost Ladybug.

Feeling better having made the decision to move forward with something, Beth relaxed and began to enjoy the drive. She'd always loved driving the Camaro. Maybe she had been a teenage boy in another life, she thought, laughing inwardly. Nothing like a good muscle car on an open road. The weather was grand, a beautiful late winter day. Beth rolled her window half way down and let the tangy fragrance of pine and snowy moisture drift through the little car. She wished her dad were here to share the ride.

"Dad?" she called out softly. "You there?"

No response.

She picked up the cell phone and checked for a signal or even a belated message.

Nothing.

The two-lane road was twisty with curves and hairpin turns. The tall pines crowded the road on both sides stippling the surface of the pavement in alternating patterns of sunlight and shadow. Driving required all her concentration. Only once did she let her mind drift back to the apparition of the little boy she thought she'd seen on the way to the cabin two days earlier. She still had no clue as to what she'd actually seen. The trooper had promised to contact her if he had any news.

Stutter Creek started and stopped, trickled and babbled, crossed beneath the road or ran alongside it all the way to town. The Drugstore was on the west side of the street. It still sported batwing doors and wooden sidewalks. A metal historical marker planted at the corner of the quaint business boasted that the old building had been in continuous use since 1867.

Beth parked in one of the slanted spaces on Main Street. There was a hitching post in front of the drugstore, and to the right of it, one could still make out the ancient circular marks where barrels of pickles had once stood.

She straightened her spine and pushed through the swinging doors. Her dad always pretended to be an outlaw stopping in for a drink when they came here. The historical marker said the building had served as the town's saloon at one time. It still amazed her that she was walking on the very boards that Billy the Kid and Pat Garrett might have trod.

The teenage girl behind the long polished oak counter was petite and blonde. She smiled cheerfully at Beth. "Anything I can help you with?" she asked.

Beth ordered a Sarsaparilla from the soda fountain. She'd always splurged and ordered the old fashioned drink made with real syrup and soda water. Even now, she liked to watch the girl pull the pearl-colored handles on the antique fountain as she concocted the sweet, foamy drink. The little drugstore also served breakfast, plus a variety of sandwiches for lunch, and dinner.

When the waitress set the drink in front of her, Beth took a long pull from the straw and sighed, "Mmmm, just as good as always."

"So, you've been here before?" the girl asked politely.

Beth nodded. "Last summer was the first one I've missed since I was a child. My dad has a . . ." She had to stop as she realized the cabin was now hers. "I mean I have a cabin a few miles away. We used to get up here two or three times a year."

The girl was very astute. "Lost your dad, huh?" Her voice was sympathetic without sounding fake.

Beth nodded and took another pull on the straw. She didn't trust her voice.

"So sorry to hear that," the teenager said, extending her hand over the counter. "My name is Allie. I just came to work for my Uncle Joe here after I graduated last year. I'm from Pine River."

Beth grasped her hand warmly over the counter. "And how is Uncle Joe?" she asked. "He used to give me a lollipop every time I came in here when I was younger."

Allie laughed. "He still does that with kids." Her face darkened perceptibly. "He's getting up in years, you know. High blood pressure, diabetes." She smiled a little. "He still comes in at least once a day to check up on me. I like to think I'm helping out. Aunt Martha is here most of the time, too. She walked over to the Post Office a few minutes ago."

Just then an older couple came in and took a table near the back. There were only four tables in addition to the counter, so it wasn't difficult for Beth and Allie to overhear their ongoing conversation.

"Such a shame," the woman's husband said. "Just not safe anywhere anymore."

Allie was drawing glasses of ice water for the couple, obviously regulars, when her Aunt Martha came scurrying in the door waving a sheet of paper showing the black and white photo of a young woman.

"Look at this!" she blurted. Then she saw Beth and changed her tone as she grabbed her in a mini-bear hug. "Bethie, you poor girl. I heard about your dad and I am so sorry. He was always one of my favorite people." She drew back a little, took hold of Beth's chin and looked her over carefully. "So how are you doing? Huh? Why, I never saw a father and daughter as close as the two of you."

Beth had no defense. She began to blubber.

"There, there, dear," Martha patted her kindly. "Didn't mean to make you cry. Got such a big mouth on me sometimes!" She continued hugging and patting while Beth dug tissues from her purse. Allie smiled ruefully and made it a point to engage the older couple in a spirited conversation as she placed the glasses of water on their table and took their orders for club sandwiches.

When Allie returned to the counter, Martha said, "Allie, dear, can you hand me the Scotch tape? I think it's in that drawer there."

The efficient girl opened a loaf of bread with one hand while rummaging through the indicated drawer with the other. "What is that?" she asked, nodding toward the picture in her aunt's hand. She continued to work, pulling on transparent plastic gloves before toasting the bread and slicing tomatoes for the sandwiches.

"Terrible thing," Martha said, holding it up for both of them to see. "Young college girl from Pine River, gone missing night before last. On her way to work, talking to her friend on the phone then POOF, she's gone. No one's seen hide nor hair since!"

The woman at the back table, obviously listening, piped up, "That the college girl we been hearing about, Martha?"

Taping the MISSING picture to the inside of the glass door so that it faced out, Martha replied, "Yes, I just picked it up over at the post office. Don will be delivering the rest of them on his route today. The girl's family stopped there to ask about posting them around the village, and Don volunteered to take a stack himself."

The man and woman looked at each other then shook their heads. "Did you talk to the family?" the man asked.

Martha shook her own head, a look of consternation crossing her kindly face. "Oh, no . . . I wouldn't want to interfere. Looked like it might've been her sister, though. You could see the worry written all over her pretty face." She tsked and clicked her tongue as she rounded the end of the counter to wash her hands and help her niece. With her back to the room, she said, "We've all got to be so careful nowadays. Especially you, Allie, pretty young girl like you. Why, you could almost pass for twins, you and that college girl on the poster."

The gentleman from the back table spoke again, "That's true, young lady. Can't be too careful. Besides all that, I heard tell there's a new fella in town. Rented a box down at the Post Office."

"Really?" Martha sniffed. "Well, he hasn't been in here, yet. Surely he'll be by to say hello if he's planning to make his home around here." She shook her head, a gesture that indicated she was amazed that anyone could come to Stutter Creek without visiting The Drugstore. "And why would he rent a P.O. Box if he wasn't planning to stay?"

The question was obviously rhetorical. No one bothered to answer. They were likely all thinking the same thing. If the guy hadn't shown himself, but had rented a post office box, then he probably didn't want a lot of folks knowing where he lived. That was a rather chilling thought in light of the MISSING GIRL poster they'd just taped up.

Beth was fascinated by the small town gossip. She'd never realized everyone knew absolutely everything about everyone else. She'd always had her dad as a buffer. He was the one everyone chatted up when they were here. She was beginning to think she'd been quite the wallflower.

Leaving the Drugstore, she stopped and studied the picture of the beautiful young woman again. She was a lot like Allie, young, blonde, and fair. Beth felt a lump of fear forming in the pit of her stomach, and she said a silent prayer for the young woman's safety. She also hoped the big dog would be at her cabin when she returned. With him there, she would feel much safer. In light of this, she might even try to entice him to stay.

On the way out of town, she stopped at the Corner Market, topped off her gas tank, and bought a large box of Milk Bones. She didn't recognize the cashier; therefore, she didn't have to explain herself. If it had been Juanita, the owner, she would have been there a while. It was only when she was back on the road that she realized someone at the drugstore or market would probably have known where the dog belonged. However, when she checked her cell phone, she actually showed three bars so she pulled off the road into a turn-around and called Cindy.

It was so good to talk to her best friend that she deliberately left out the part about seeing the boy. She also did not tell her friend about the missing girl from Pine River. Beth did tell her all about the big dog, though. He seemed like a safe topic. She also drew Cindy into a discussion about the afterlife.

Turned out Cindy wasn't the least bit surprised when Beth admitted she thought her Dad's spirit was still around. "Oh, you just wouldn't believe the strange happenings some of my patients have told me about after their loved ones passed away," Cindy related. "Footsteps in the hall, lights that went on by themselves, cold drafts . . ."

Beth came very close to telling Cindy the whole truth, cell phone and all. But something held her back. Maybe because she was afraid of how it would sound when she actually said it out loud.

After a few minutes, the two hung up. "I'll try to call you again in a day or two," Beth told her. "But don't worry if I don't. Remember, I have to drive almost all the way down the mountain before I can get a signal."

Chapter Fifteen

A New Mexico State Trooper found Amanda's car two days after she was reported missing. The investigators were not surprised to find lots of different prints in the car of a college student. However, they were somewhat perplexed when a few of those prints appeared to belong to a child, especially since they were very fresh, and only in the back of the vehicle.

"So it looks like she was telling the truth when she called her friend at work," the senior detective muttered to her rookie partner.

They looked at each other.

Woody James agreed with a nod. "Puts a whole new light on the case."

Senior Detective Kendra Dean plopped down at her desk, slipped her reading glasses on, and reread the initial report. The two of them had just returned from impound where they'd watched forensics process the vehicle.

She nodded absently as she read everything she'd just witnessed. As she nodded, her hair moved back and forth. She'd been a detective long enough to know that when you're called out at three a.m., hair and makeup were the last things you wanted to worry about, but as it brushed her ears, she knew she needed it cut again. The short, carefree hair and lack of makeup completely suited her no nonsense personality.

"Obviously killed in the car—"

Detective James looked up. "What makes you say that? We don't have a body yet."

Kendra Dean barely shrugged. "Didn't you see the condition of that dash? The hair all over the place? Someone put up one hell of a struggle. Some of that hair appeared to have been ripped out by the roots." She waited for the younger detective to catch up with her thinking, to visualize it in his head the way she had. "Someone came in the passenger side, grabbed her, she put up a good fight, kicked hell out of the underside of the dash, he grabbed her by the hair, smashed her head against the window and—"

James nodded. "Okay. Yeah, I see what you mean." They were both appalled by the obvious violence that had occurred inside the victim's car. "But what makes you so sure she isn't still alive somewhere?" His raised eyebrows and crinkled forehead told the senior detective that he wasn't being a smartass, just trying to understand.

Kendra leaned back in her chair. She pushed her reading glasses up on her head. "Imagine you're the perp: he wants the woman bad enough to go into her car, probably using the kid as bait—"

Det. James started to interrupt, but Kendra held up one hand and continued.

"—she puts up a struggle, he has to get control. What's he do? Hit her? Drag her out of the car, what?"

Woody James thought carefully before answering. "He didn't hit her; not much anyway. Not that much blood."

Dean nodded encouragingly.

"So," he continued. "He gets control quickly, maybe by using the kid as leverage, you know. Do what I say or the kid gets it . . ."

"That's possible," she agreed. "But I don't really see it that way."

He waited.

"We don't have anything that puts the kid in the front seat of the car. Kid, probably a boy according to what the victim told her friend, was only in the back, if the prints are correct, and I think they are. But Amanda, she was all over the front seat and the front floorboard."

James nodded. He'd forgotten about the floorboard. There had been more hair and fibers there; smears of semen on the front seat. Detective James shook his head as images of the young woman's pain and terror flooded his mind. "I see what you're saying, now. No way she lived through that kind of a struggle without shedding a lot of blood. Strangulation then?"

Nodding absently, Kendra slipped her glasses back in place on the bridge of her nose. "Can't be sure, of course. But I say we get that cadaver dog back out here. Time to start searching for a body."

Detective James tapped his pencil against the report. "I sure hope you're wrong—no offense, of course. In that case, what do we tell the family?"

"Nothing," she snorted. "We don't know anything for sure. It's all speculation. Get that dog up here, but don't splatter it across the news. Tell the state boys to come in quietly." She peered over her half-moon glasses at the young man itching to do something. "Just remember, one dead girl is a news report; two dead girls will mean serial killer headlines." She took the glasses off, laid them on the desk. "We're not ready for headlines, yet."

"So you really think the arm case in Yellow Bend is related to this one?" the young detective asked.

"Let's hope not," Detective Dean replied. "But the press will think so, that I can almost guarantee." She turned back to the report. "Can't wait to get that DNA report. I'll bet money that creep is already in the system. Too bad there were no fingerprints. We'd have him already."

***

Shaniqua Patterson hung up the phone. "Fired," she said. "That girl is so fired." She pulled Sherylyn's time card from the stack and headed toward the night manager's office.

Rapping hard with her closed knuckles, she pushed the metal office door open and entered speaking: "Ms. Deevy, I can't reach Sherylyn on the phone. This the second day she hadn't showed up. I'ma go ahead and pull in Dewayne, that part-timer. He's been wantin' full time. I'm givin' him Sherylyn's shift." She started out the door without waiting for approval.

Candy Deevy nodded, barely raising her fingers from the keyboard. "Good decision. That's what I pay you for," she murmured.

Then a brief memory flashed across her mind. The memory was of Sherylyn talking to a friend in the cashier's meeting last week. She'd been going on and on about the possibility of moving closer to work so she wouldn't have so far to drive. She had seemed pretty excited about an apartment that was opening up, even talked about the new apartment having a balcony, said she was looking forward to getting a grill with her employee discount. Doesn't sound like someone who suddenly quits for no reason, Candy Deevy thought. The girl had plans.

"Hey," she called before the door closed.

Shaniqua stuck her head back in, a question framing her features.

"You got an emergency contact number?"

"Tried it," the cashier-manager said bluntly, pulling her head back through the door as if the matter was closed.

"Try it again," Ms. Deevy ordered. "In fact, send someone to her house. Better yet, you got her landlord's number?"

On the other side of the door, Shaniqua looked at her watch and rolled her eyes. Sherylyn's shift started an hour ago. Her register was closed, lines were backing up, and customers were getting cranky. Taking a deep, calming breath, she cracked the door open again. "I don't have landlord's numbers. Think she lived in a duplex."

The night manager sat upright at her battered gunmetal gray desk, her fingers poised over the computer keyboard. "Find out if she's got a friend that'll check out her place. If not, keep trying the contact number. I've got a feeling she didn't just not come to work. Might've been in a car wreck or something. Can't be too careful, you know."

Shaniqua's feet hurt. She wasn't a small woman; and she still had seven hours to go on her own shift. "Yes, ma'am," she sighed. "I'll see what we can do." Then she shuffled out into the hall shaking her head. She still had to get in touch with Dewayne, too. *Hell, maybe I should have him go by Sherylyn's house. Nah, him I need on the line, now.*

***

Kurt and Danny had finally found the cave. It was on the lower slope of Blue Mountain, the entrance almost completely hidden by brush.

It's cold at night in the mountains. In March and April, the weather is very unpredictable. Warm temperatures in the daytime can slide right down below freezing when the sun sets.

Danny was cold all the time. Kurt let him lie near the door in the sunshine. "Soak up some rays," he said jovially. "Just keep your mouth shut."

He didn't have to worry about Danny calling out to anyone. There wasn't anyone this high on the mountain. Besides, the boy was both sick and drugged. He didn't know night from day. He barely even noticed when darkness fell. All he knew was that he was cold and thirsty.

That night, Kurt wrapped him in the nylon tent and stowed him in the corner of the dank cave like a box of old clothes. He wasn't ready to lose his bait. But Danny was already so ill he could barely raise his head.

Kurt wanted to move on as soon as he'd dealt with the owner of the Camaro and his Stutter Creek victim. But he knew if his bait died, his plan would be much harder to complete. And without the plan, he was afraid he would implode. Besides, just like heroin, killing was addictive. He couldn't wait for his next fix.

He thought if he could get the kid some better food and some dry clothes, maybe the boy would last long enough for him to finish his list. He wasn't ready to give up just yet. The first girls had been too much fun. But five was the magic number. Five girls for five years. The old broad would just be one-to-grow-on. He thought of putting that in the letter to the prosecutor. Definitely have to remember to put that in there, he thought, but first: have to get the kid some decent food and a source of warmth. Maybe the owner of the Camaro would share that toasty little cabin if he asked her just right.

He grinned.

He knew just how he would ask her.

Kurt began making preparations right away. First, he gave Danny another dose of drugs to knock him out completely. He didn't want him to panic in the night and come stumbling down the mountain so he tied his hands and feet together just in case he awoke. He thought briefly of the possibility of a bear or mountain lion coming into the cave and finding the boy trussed up like a Christmas goose, but he pushed that thought away immediately. What happens, happens, he thought. Some things were beyond human control. Hadn't the prison psychologist told him that over and over again? Only worry about things you can change; don't waste your energy on things beyond your control. Another idiot. The psycho-ologist seemed to think Kurt was some sort of misunderstood genius who had self-medicated with drugs because of his awful upbringing.

He laughed every time he thought of how he'd buffaloed her. She wasn't blonde like the prosecutor, but she was every bit as annoying.

Besides, nothing was going to happen to Danny. They had Fate on their side. On the other hand, so what if it did? The kid was sick anyway. It would just hasten the inevitable. Maybe I'll even steal another kid, little girl next time. Getting Danny certainly hadn't been a problem.

Kurt shrugged and started down the mountain to figure out the best way to get inside the cabin. He planned to be nearby when Beth went to sleep tonight. If he couldn't get inside before she went to bed, he planned to be near enough that he could hear her snoring when she went under. Only this time, it would be a long sleep, one from which she would not awaken.

Chapter Sixteen

It wasn't difficult to find someone willing to drive to Sherylyn's house to check up on her. Apparently, she had been friendly, but not close, with several coworkers. When Shaniqua pointed out that she had not been to work in a couple of days, a few people offered to drive over and check on her.

Two of them begged to go together just in case they found something so grisly they would have to hold each other up while they dialed 911 on one of their cell phones.

Shaniqua began to wonder if they weren't really hoping to find something awful so they would have something to tell in the break room tomorrow. Nonetheless, she let them take off work an hour early so they could check it out.

"And don't forget to call me when you find out what's going on," she reminded them sternly. "I don't hear from you before I get off, I'll dock you for that hour I let you go. Got it?"

They got it.

But it didn't matter. Sherylyn's car was not there, no lights were on, and no one was home on the other side of the duplex.

"Ain't she got no fam'ly?" Carol asked Kevin as they stood on the porch of the rundown little home.

"Search me," he replied. "I just came along so you wouldn't have to identify her dead body all by yourself. You see anything in that window?"

Carol bent over and peered through the dusty glass of the front window. "Nah, curtains are in the way. Can't make out nothing. Let's try the back."

The back door was locked up tight, and all the curtains were drawn on that side of the house, too.

Walking back around the house, Kevin had an idea. "Hey, let's see if she's got mail piling up."

Carol shrugged. "Might tell us if she's in town or out of town, I guess."

But there was no way to tell. Both sides of the duplex were equipped with mail slots beside their front doors. Kevin tried to see through it, but it was designed to prevent peepers, and it worked.

In the end, no one found out what had become of Sherylyn. No one reported her missing because they assumed she had driven away in her own car.

Shaniqua hired Dewayne who was thrilled to be able to work one full time job with benefits instead of two part-time jobs without.

Ms. Deevy never thought about her again. After all, she had all those other night people to manage. Later, she would have a few qualms of guilt over how easily the unfortunate girl had slipped everyone's mind.

***

Beth was famished by the time she got back to the cabin. She had really intended to order a sandwich to go with her drink at the drugstore; however, the news of the missing girl and the ensuing gossip had made her completely forget her hunger, until now.

She pulled into the circle drive and shut off the engine. In the back of her mind, she wondered if her dad had gone on. She glanced down at her cell phone. *Did I really communicate with him?* Now, after a bit of time had passed, it seemed ludicrous. Still, she vowed to try again inside the cabin. For some reason, texting with the dead seemed easier in secret—or at least out of the public eye. She laughed self-consciously. There was no one around for miles. Shivering as much from nerves as from the chill, Beth felt very exposed standing beside the car in the driveway. Cocking her head slightly, she listened for any noise that might herald the arrival of the giant dog.

The only sounds she heard were bird related, and the incessant breeze high up in the tall pines.

She gave up on seeing the dog again, and went on inside the cabin where she immediately lit a fire. A smoky scent invaded the room before she had the fire going.

"Dad, you still here?"

Colored lights immediately darted around her face. They lasted only a few seconds, and then the phone beeped.

STILL HERE. YOU OK?

"Sure." She opened the fridge for sliced cheese and whipped butter. "I'm fine." She retrieved the cast iron skillet from the drawer beneath the stove. "Just got back from the drugstore—"

MARTHA AND JOE OK?

Beth set the skillet on the stove and buttered two slices of bread. One slice went butter side down in the skillet with a slice of pepper jack cheese on top, and then the second slice of bread closed it up. In a few minutes she would flip the sandwich over so both sides were evenly toasted and the cheese gooey and melted. This was more of her comfort food.

"Martha's doing great, Joe's having health problems. He wasn't even there. They've got his niece—"

ALLIE.

"That's right! I can't believe you remember her name."

JUST A LITTLE THING LAST TIME I SAW HER.

"Well, she is a beautiful young woman, now." She thought briefly about the poster of the missing girl who looked so much like Allie; but then she decided he didn't need to know about that. Even as she was doing it, Beth couldn't believe she was trying to protect her father's spirit from worrying about her. She guessed some things never changed. For her father to worry, that had always been a no-no to her.

"Dad—"

BETH—

They both began to speak/write at the same time.

YOU FIRST, he wrote.

"I just wish you were here to eat a toasty cheese sandwich with me."

SIGHING. ME TOO. BUT NO ONE GOES BACK. EVERYONE MOVES FORWARD. SOME FASTER THAN OTHERS. WINK WINK.

"Oh, Dad. You're still crazy—"

AFTER ALL THESE YEARS.

"Did I tell you I love you?" she asked.

MANY TIMES. NOW, WHEN ARE YOU HEADING BACK? IT'S ABOUT TIME YOU GOT ON WITH YOUR LIFE. TAKING CARE OF ABBY AND MY UPCOMING GREAT-GRANDKIDS.

Beth stopped in mid-chew. "Do you know something I don't?"

JUST HOPEFUL, he replied. WILL YOU TELL THEM ALL ABOUT ME? PLEASE?

Setting aside her sandwich, Beth said, "Dad, even if you are a figment of my imagination, surely you know how I will regale them with tales of their great-grandfather." She could not continue, her voice was stuck in her throat, and it wasn't because of the sandwich.

SORRY, BABY. THAT WAS STUPID OF ME. I NEVER WANT TO MAKE YOU CRY. I KEEP FORGETTING YOU ARE STILL THERE—IT IS SO

DIFFERENT NOW. NO SADNESS. NO
HEARTACHE.

"Can't you tell me more?" she asked softly, tears
thickening her voice.

NOT WITH WORDS, he said. THERE SIMPLY
AREN'T ANY WORDS TO DESCRIBE IT. MAYBE
BECAUSE IF THERE WERE, EVRYONE WOULD
COME TOO EARLY.

"You mean earth would be empty?"

VERY POSSIBLY.

Beth thought he was being serious; but it was way too
big to wrap her head around. It reminded her of the time a
professor had told their class about the theory of the
universe expanding like a rubber band, and that someday it
would reach its limit and snap back. Without thinking Beth
had blurted, "Would that make time move backward?" He
must have sensed that she was not being facetious—even
though, later, she felt kind of silly for blurting out such a
juvenile question—for he replied, kindly, "Could be, who
knows?"

She swallowed another bite of her sandwich. "How
long before you move on?"

TOMORROW, SUNRISE. I THINK YOU'RE
STRONG ENOUGH.

She felt flattened, as if she had just became a cardboard
cut-out of herself. But I'll be strong, for Dad, she thought.
He said I wouldn't mind him leaving this time because he
would be going to find Mom. That's what I'll focus on.

"Will you come and say goodbye before you go?"

CALL MY NAME WHEN YOU WAKE UP. I'LL BE
WAITING.

"Love you," she whispered.

The tiny Christmassy lights sparkled around her face,
and were gone.

***

Kurt couldn't believe his ears. Would she never shut up and get off the phone? She had been chatting for twenty minutes, yet he couldn't see the phone. She appeared to be just carrying it around and looking at it. She wasn't texting; she was talking out loud. Must have it on speaker, or maybe she was wearing one of those headsets or something. He watched carefully for a few more minutes. It was easy to track her movements as she moved around in the small cabin.

After a few bites of the sandwich, he'd seen her move slowly from kitchen to living area, straightening and turning off lights as she went. He even saw her bank the fire and check the front door; probably to see if it was locked, Kurt thought. Next would be the bedroom. When that light goes out, that's when I'll make my move. She'll never know what hit her.

He didn't notice the tiny darting lights that flickered briefly in the darkened cabin. Nor did he notice when those same lights melted into the gloom of the forest. Kurt was too focused on his prize to notice much of anything. He was tired of sleeping cold. Even prison hadn't been this cold and damp. Tonight, I'll be warm and toasty, just like that fragrant sandwich. Warm and toasty.

Inside the cabin, Beth brushed her teeth. She felt very tired, like she might actually sleep. Last night hadn't been too bad, once she had finally fallen asleep, that is. Tonight, she planned to look over some of the novel-notes she'd written over the years. Maybe she would even add a few words to them. She'd forgotten how quickly night fell in the mountains. The days seemed so short.

If she had trouble concentrating on her writing, she could always read some more of those gossip magazines. She might even start on the paperback novel she had brought. It was a John Grisham. She had pointedly avoided bringing anything scary or romantic. Those two genres were off limits for a while—maybe forever.

Outside the cabin, Kurt eased onto the porch and sat with his back against the rail. His knees were cold and aching from kneeling on the hummock across from the picture window. All at once he became aware of a low growling coming from the woods behind the cabin. He had a moment to realize how strange it was that he could hear the growl before he could hear or see any movement.

Slowly he worked his way to a standing position without making a sound. Very carefully, he peered around the corner of the cabin. In the darkness, he could make out the black shape of some large animal that appeared to be creeping toward him.

"Down!" a deep voice commanded in a whisper.

The animal sank immediately to the ground.

The low growl continued.

Kurt stepped off the front of the porch and began to work his way back toward the cave. Keeping to the deep shadows cast by the cabin's overhang, he didn't think the man could see him; and the dog, if indeed that's what the humongous creature was, could probably only smell him.

As much as he hated to be even colder, Kurt decided he would take a circular path back to the cave, walking at least part of the way in the creek to cover his tracks. He'd picked that up from an old western, too.

John strained to see what Turk was growling about. Not an animal. He'd been trained not to alert at animal scents. Had to be a person. Can't let him take down just anyone in the National Forest, John thought. Could be a camper, a hiker, or even a Forest Ranger. He knelt beside Turk and scanned the area with his field glasses.

He saw nothing. Together, man and dog stood and made their way down to the little cabin. In the darkness, John could not see the footprints. But he knew something wasn't right. Turk wouldn't alert at a person inside a cabin. And if there was someone outside, why were they hiding? No one should be skulking around the forest in the darkness. We'll get to the bottom of this tomorrow, he thought. No need to scare the cabin's new owners this late in the evening.

On the way back to his own place, John swatted at the swarm of fireflies still flickering around his face. They'd been with him now, off and on, since the moment he'd started hiking back toward his own cabin after locating Turk. The dog had taken to disappearing about sunset each night. John didn't know what was causing the strange behavior, but he assumed it was simply the abundance of wildlife in the area.

The mutt was stuck to his heel, now, though. Which is what he was trained to do. But both times John had been forced to go out and find him; Turk had been near the Brannock's old cabin.

Tramping along, he let his mind wander back to the summer he'd spent with Beth and Tom Brannock, but those memories were too painful. He pushed them away and continued up the mountain toward his own home.

If he hadn't been so deep in thought, John might have noticed that the fireflies were still with him, and that they came in quite a variety of colors.

All at once, something convinced John to change his course. The more he thought about it, the stranger it seemed for Turk to return to this cabin each night. The fact that he alerted at something just now was very odd, too.

John had been doing his best not to see bad guys at every turn. But his military training was so well ingrained that he had convinced himself that he would have to start making a conscious effort to relax and not be on guard all the time.

Nevertheless, Turk was acting too strange.

And the fact that they were in the forest didn't mean they were completely safe. No matter how much he'd thought that it would.

He decided they should keep a watch at the cabin overnight, just in case. He wasn't sure why, but he chalked it up to intuition. Big John was a firm believer in listening to that inner voice. Especially at night, in the middle of the woods.

He swatted at the fireflies again, but he wasn't really seeing them. Mostly, they were just a colorful nuisance.

Chapter Seventeen

"A flat?" Janie could not believe it. For a moment, she suspected Ray of concocting the story just to get her in trouble. He was always teasing her about being a "goody two shoes," and then he would threaten to keep her out past her curfew just to see how much trouble she would really be in. Janie wondered if this was what her mom had meant about "resisting the lure of bad boys." She just hoped he would get her home soon so she could tell him she never wanted to see him again. She was beginning to think this was the night he was going to make good on his silly teasing threats.

When she heard him coming back, Janie glanced up, angry, disbelieving. Ray was such a throwback. He was almost ridiculously good looking, the quintessential tall dark and handsome player. When he popped open the door latch and plopped back down in the driver's seat to light a cigarette, Janie wondered, not for the first time, why he was even with her. He was already out of school with a full time job in his uncle's garage, and here she was, just a sophomore band geek. So far, he had treated her with grudging respect, but now . . . a flat tire on a deserted back road? Wasn't that just a little bit too cliché?

She watched as he inhaled and exhaled lazily. "Shouldn't you be changing the tire?" she finally asked.

Ray smiled and let the smoke curl out of his lips and upward into his nostrils before he spoke. "Spare's flat, too."

Janie felt a sinking sensation in the pit of her stomach. Without thinking, she opened the passenger door and stepped out into the night. They were on some rural road south of Pine River. She wasn't really sure where they were. They had just gone for a drive, listening to music. Wasting gas, Ray called it, as in, "Hey Baby, wanna go waste some gasoline?" He'd said that to her the first time she met him at a party in Yellow Bend. She wasn't supposed to be there, and he knew it. She had talked her older cousin into inviting her. Ray had taken her away before she'd finished her first beer.

Surprisingly, he had been a perfect, albeit wiseass, gentleman. And she'd gotten home on time, and in one piece. But this was their third "date." Perhaps he was tired of playing nice with Little Miss Goody-two-shoes.

Janie stood beside the Mustang for a few seconds trying to decide what she should do. She needed a cell phone. Her parents wouldn't let her have one because some kids at school had created a big stir when they were caught sexting. Besides, Ray was her first "real" boyfriend. All the others had been just friends, or group things. And someone in the group always had a phone. I'll have one after this, she promised herself as she stomped around trying to decide what to do. One way or another!

"Finally alone . . ." Ray said as he stepped out of the driver's door and started around the front of the car. "Time to ravish the fair maiden!" He laughed evilly, like the bad guy in a cartoon. "Muahahaha!"

Janie panicked. She had intended to simply start walking back toward town, but once her feet were in motion, they took over and she began to run. All at once, the road curved and she didn't. As she stumbled down into the bar ditch, she glanced back. That's when she noticed the red flashers on the Mustang. Would he have turned those on if he had planned something terrible? Was he really just teasing? Her inexperienced brain told her it was a distinct possibility, but by then, she was scrambling up the other side of the ditch, and she didn't have the breath to ask.

"Janie!" he called. "What the hell?" His boots clunked across the pavement and then thunked when they hit the hard packed earth of the shoulder.

That sound meant he was coming for her. Janie began to run again. She couldn't seem to help herself. Mesquite thorns grabbed at her jeans, and she prayed she wouldn't fall into a clump of prickly pear. It grew so low to the ground it was almost impossible to see, even with the half-light of the moon. In the back of her mind, a thought was forming. Wasn't it illegal to go off and leave a car with the engine running? Hadn't she heard that somewhere? Or was it just another one of those fallacies like not driving barefoot or you could get arrested for prostitution. And what did it matter? Then it hit her—he had the flashers on so people could see them. If he was going to do anything bad he definitely wouldn't have put on the flash—

Janie's thoughts were abruptly cut off as the earth dropped out from under her. "Ooofff," she said as the breath whooshed out of her lungs without warning.

Ray, a few steps behind her, immediately realized what had spooked her. He'd clowned around too many times about ravishing her and then sending her home to daddy. It was all a joke. He was only showing off, delighting in the way her eyes would get big and she would giggle girlishly. Sometimes he forgot what a kid she really was. He was just so damned infatuated with her.

"Janie" His voice held an edge of panic. She had disappeared right under his nose. "Janie! Answer me dammit!"

When the toe of his boot met thin air and he had to pinwheel his arms to keep from falling into the void, Ray knew what had happened. Even as his thoughts caught up with his feet, a blood freezing scream split the night wide open.

Ray didn't hesitate; his cowboy boots slipped and slid as his hands grabbed for something, anything, on the loose-rock slope of the arroyo. All the way down he was muttering, "I'm coming. Hold on, I'm coming." Horrific images were rotating through his mind as he slid and tumbled to the bottom of the steep ravine: mountain lion, cactus, mountain lion, cactus, mountain lion, bear? Could a bear have gotten this far from the mountains? "Janie!" he bellowed again when his feet hit level ground. "Where are you?"

"Here," she whispered. "I'm over here, Ray."

That's when he saw her.

The other girl.

She was at the bottom of the arroyo, her legs and arms all akimbo as if she had slid down the slope and come to rest with her neck bent at an angle that denied the possibility of life. Her clothes were also askew—blouse hiked up, pants all twisted. It was the most horrifying thing he'd ever seen. Even in the scant light of the moon, they could see the unnatural bloat and color of the young woman's face.

He looked at Janie. She was simply staring. Pointing and staring. Her beautiful auburn hair hung in messy strands about her face, her jeans were torn on both knees, and her hand was simply hanging there in space, pointing at the dead girl on the ground.

Ray grabbed her and spun her around so she couldn't look anymore. He pulled her to his side and started slowly back up the slope. He would have given anything if Janie hadn't seen that. She was too young. Hell, he was too young; in fact, no one was old enough to see something like that. He wondered if the killer was still in the area. His macho side half-wished he was. Wouldn't he like to have a go at the monster that did that? On the other hand, he would be lucky if he could get Janie back to the car before one of them started bawling, or worse yet, barfing.

***

Kurt sat, shivering, in the mouth of the cave. His anger was a live thing pounding inside his skull, trying to hammer its way out. He was soaking wet, colder than ever, and his plan was getting all screwed up. Something had to give. For one brief second, he thought of abandoning the plan and pitching Danny into the dark abyss at the rear of the cave. He was pretty sure no one would ever find him; in fact, that abyss was where he intended to dispose of the old bitch down there in the cabin. It was pitch black and so deep it was practically bottomless.

But if he gave up and abandoned the plan . . . what would he do? He had nothing else to do, no place to go. The plan was his life. He had to get back to it. His blonde girls were waiting. He put his hand inside his coat pocket and felt for the list of names. Just touching them made him feel better. Everything was not lost.

"Tomorrow," he muttered. I get her tomorrow or I get the hell out. The plan was all that he had been living for; but now, in this cold, wet cave, he was remembering how sweet that Mexican brown had looked going into Dave's arm. And the expression on Dave's face, well, it had been a long time since Kurt had felt that way—wasted and floating—and now he was beginning to remember. He was beginning to long for the blank feeling of euphoria.

As he sat just inside the cave's entrance, cursing his luck, Kurt recalled how a counselor in prison had said one of the main reasons heroin was so addictive was that no matter how much a person used, it was impossible to replicate that first time. He said junkies would keep trying for that feeling—using more and more and more—until the drug killed them. Or until someone locked them up and made them quit against their will, Kurt thought. Then it occurred to him that since it had been so long since he'd used, the next time he "imbibed" would be just like the first. Maybe even better.

And in his wonderland of drug-dreams, he must have dozed, for the next thing he knew; he was gazing out at the light of day. He could hear Danny in the corner. His breathing was ragged and thick. It has to be today or tonight. He knew this would be the last job he did with his son. Kurt hoped the little brat could even hold on that long—he knew the woman wouldn't turn down the kid again, especially when she saw how sick he was.

He stood and stretched the kinks out of his joints. He needed dry clothes or he would soon be in the same shape Danny was in. There are lots of empty summer cabins around here, he thought. Just have to stay on this side of the mountain, near the road. That's where most people settled. Very few wanted to really walk on the wild side; they just liked to pretend.

Kurt left the cave and made his way down the mountain at a leisurely pace. He prided himself on his ability to move stealthily through the forest.

Within minutes he was in sight of the road leading to the village of Stutter Creek. Of course he knew the name of the town; it was the place where his next victim lived. This one he had found on Facebook. She wasn't really from Stutter Creek, but her update said she was going to be "spending the summer helping out at the Drugstore in Stutter Creek."

Bingo! He had accepted the "invitation" gladly. There was only one drugstore in Stutter Creek. And from the Google maps he had spent so much time studying, he figured there were bound to be some still-empty vacation houses there. Or there could be someone with laundry hanging on a clothesline; he'd seen more and more of that the closer he got to the woods and the lake. Kurt wasn't picky. It didn't have to fit like a glove; it just had to be dry.

Nope, his plan wasn't dead, it was just on hold. In fact, if Fate was still with him, he might be able to follow the plan and take care of the other, too. It would be click, click, click, like dominos falling one after the other. He didn't care which came first, the old broad with the Camaro, or the pretty little blonde at the drugstore. Afterward, he'd dispose of Danny, too.

It would all be solved tonight. He'd gotten bogged down when he'd varied from the plan the night he'd first watched the Camaro judder to a stop beside the highway. Never should have sent Danny over—got caught up in the possibility of an unscheduled high—but it didn't matter now. Soon, all his problems would be solved, and he'd be back on track.

He continued tramping along the road toward Stutter Creek, stepping behind a tree if he heard a car coming. Kurt had hidden Dave's car in the forest, he was certain old Dave would be missing it by now. Best to leave it parked where it was. Sure couldn't risk some countie-mountie seeing it if Dave had reported it stolen.

As luck would have it, he stumbled upon a nice little cabin just on the outskirts of town. The cabin itself appeared to be protected by a Sentinel Security system, but the detached garage was not. There were no vehicles in the garage, not even the customary 4-wheel drive Mule or Gator that most summer people favored; but lo and behold, there were some clothes hanging on a hook just inside the unlocked door. Apparently someone had hung them there to dry and then forgot about them. Maybe they, too, had taken an unexpected dip in the creek.

Judging by the Rolling Stones logo on the t-shirt, that someone was probably a teenager just about his size, or a middle-aged man who refused to grow up. Could even be a woman for all he knew. Men's and women's jeans and t-shirts were pretty much interchangeable, and Kurt wasn't a large man.

He stripped quickly and pulled on the dry clothing. The idea that it could belong to a woman, or girl, excited him. The clothes were a perfect fit. The word Fate flashed through his mind, but he didn't say it out loud for fear of jinxing the whole thing. He zipped his jacket up to cover the big red mouth and tongue logo on the t-shirt, and then he hung his own wet pants and shirt on the hook. He was glad his jacket was waterproof. For a moment he wished he could be a fly on the wall when the previous owner of the Stones tee went back to retrieve it and found Kurt's old thrift store shirt in its place.

Chapter Eighteen

Allie flipped the radio to the local top-forty station and turned it up. Kings of Leon, her favorite band. She loved their energy, and the way they could make the strangest words sound so . . . melodic. Her Uncle Joe said she was going to ruin her hearing if she wasn't careful. But like most teens, Allie thought he worried just a little too much. Reaching over to crank it up another notch, she flew around the hairpin turns with ease. She'd been driving these roads every summer since the day she got her license.

When she reached the drugstore, she noticed a slender man lounging near the light pole at the corner of the building. He was leaned forward a bit at the waist, and he seemed to be studying the Missing Girl poster on the front door of the Drugstore. His face was in shadow, his eyes nothing more than dark wells in a slightly lighter plane of flesh. He stood with one leg cocked so that the foot on that side rested flat against the wall behind him. Apparently, he didn't have a care in the world, just reading the poster as a way to pass the time.

Allie watched him for a second before turning off the street and into the parking area behind the drugstore. Just reading the poster. Probably a tourist waiting for someone. That wouldn't be unusual; lots of folks used the Drugstore as a meeting place. It was only one of two businesses open this early in the morning. The other being The Corner Store. And since Martha put up the poster, lots of folks had stopped for a second and sometimes a third look before going on about their business.

She parked her uncle's faded blue Chevy Lumina in the alley space behind the store and got out to unlock the drugstore's rear entrance. The silence after the loud music was deafening. Allie smiled, glad that her Aunt had trusted her enough to get things ready to open for the day. Her Uncle Joe's emphysema had seemed worse this morning, and she was glad she could be there to help.

At noon, Martha drove up to the drugstore in her little Toyota Celica. She was so thankful that Allie was staying with them to help out. Martha had no idea what she would do when the girl decided she'd had enough of small town life and was ready to tackle college. Best not to think of that now. One day at a time, that's what she would concentrate on. One day at a time.

After the lunch run, Martha helped Allie clean up. Then she told the girl to take the rest of the day off. "You've been here since seven a.m.," she said. "It's time you go out and have some fun. You're only supposed to be part time anyhow." She clucked her tongue. "Go on, now. Skedaddle!" The older woman slapped a rolled up cup towel at her behind jokingly.

Allie smiled. She knew her Aunt was serious, as if she could just run out and start having fun because her aunt told her to. In Stutter Creek, there wasn't much to do between the seasons. It wasn't like in a city where one could visit a mall or take in an afternoon matinee. Nope, ski season was over, and it would be a few more weeks before families would start arriving in droves with their shiny new tents and canoes strapped to the tops of their SUVs.

However, there were a couple things she'd not had time for lately. One was trying on new clothes. Summer was just around the corner and all her shorts were raggedy, skin tight, or just downright ugly. She also wanted a new bathing suit. It seemed premature to be thinking of a swimsuit with patches of snow still on the ground, but she'd visited Stutter Creek every summer since she could remember. She knew what spring was like in the mountains; freezing cold one day with snow spitting angrily at the greenery brave enough to show its new colors, then the next day might climb to 75 or 80 degrees before noon. After that, swimming weather would be upon them without warning. Besides, roasting marshmallows over a campfire didn't always entail actually getting in the water.

In the summer she practically lived at the lake, and last year's suit was so . . . childish. This year, she felt brave enough for a bikini, or at least one of those tankini things. She could even see herself toasting marshmallows at the lake in a new suit with one of those colorful sarongs to wrap up in when she felt too self-conscious.

Maybe Ginger would be home by now. She attended college three days a week in Pine River. She planned to teach kindergarten someday. Miller's Outlet, one of the two clothing stores in town—the other being Wes's Western Wear—might be putting out their summer stuff. If not, perhaps the two of them could meet up before Ginger left the city. Aunt Martha was right, she did need to get out and have some fun.

***

After her sandwich, and the conversation with her dad, Beth felt restless. She decided to go for a short hike, to clear her head. Outside, in the fresh air, things always seemed better. She stopped just outside her property line in the edge of the woods. The soft sunlight was filtering down through the pine canopy like golden rain. She admired the falling light, thinking what a lovely painting it would make, and how hard it would be to get the light just right—she'd tried her hand at watercolors in college—when she heard a tiny sound like a small animal snuffling around in the leaves.

Turning carefully, not wanting to frighten a deer or perhaps even a fox, just wanting to catch a glimpse of it, she was treated to . . . nothing. Gestalt, she thought; go gestalt, like Dad always said. Look at the whole forest and see what doesn't fit. Don't look at the individual trees; look at the patterns of dark and light. Look for something that breaks the pattern . . .

Still, there was nothing. Everything seemed to be in its correct place.

Slowly she turned around again. There! Another noise. This time it sounded like feet sliding on soft earth. Goose pimples appearing on the backs of her arms, she whirled around counterclockwise and caught a spot of movement. Her blood momentarily froze, rooting her feet to the spot; then anger boiled up and spilled over.

"Come out, dammit! I know you're there. You've been watching me and I'm sick of it! Come out where I can see you—coward!"

A dozen yards away, a man stepped out from behind a towering ponderosa pine. Beside him, alert and imposing, stood the large dog that had come to visit her.

Beth stamped her foot, nostrils flaring, eyes flashing. She wasn't frightened. She was mad. She wanted to speak but her breath was trapped in her throat. To get it out she would have to start yelling.

"Sorry," the man said, holding on to the dog's collar. "We didn't mean to startle you; in fact, I was trying to let you pass on by so that we wouldn't startle you." He looked down at the dog affectionately. "But old Turk here seems to have forgotten everything I taught him about surveillance—"

As if on cue Turk pulled from his grasp and leaped straight at Beth. The man opened his mouth as if to halt the huge dog, but before he could utter a word, Beth was on one knee, arms open wide.

He raised one eyebrow suspiciously. "So," he said. "You've corrupted my ferocious guard dog." He slid the sunglasses off his nose and hooked them onto the neck of his shirt as he spoke.

Beth's gasp was audible. "John?" Her voice was incredulous. "Big John, is that you?" She couldn't believe her eyes. After all these years of searching, looking for him in the shade of every evergreen, poking around his slowly crumbling cabin like a thief, leaving surreptitious notes tied with hair ribbons that blew away on the first strong breeze. . .after all that, here he was standing in the middle of the forest not fifty feet from her back door. Her heart seemed to be walloping the inside of her chest like a velvet-covered hammer. Her tongue was stranded in the desert of her mouth. She couldn't seem to work up enough spittle to form any more words.

Beth looked him over closely. His blond hair was short, beginning to gray; a soft, close-trimmed beard covered the lower half of his face; his clothes were camouflage; and his eyes, the sea-glass green eyes that had haunted her memories all through the years, were staring at her as if they'd never seen her before.

Finally, she blurted out: "So you're the owner of this magnificent animal who has been taking such good care of me?" *Get a grip, Beth. You're not a teenager anymore.*

The tall man ducked his head and muttered. "Guilty on both counts."

Beth thought he might be blushing, but beneath the shade of the pines, it was difficult to tell. Finally, when she could breathe again, she whispered, "Don't you know me? It's Beth, Beth Brannock, I mean, Evans. You know, Tom Brannock's girl."

She might have gone on and on identifying herself but John finally held up his hand. "Of course I know you, Bethie. I'd know you anywhere." His gaze was direct, his voice kind. "Can't believe you're here, that's all." Then he grinned, his eyes crinkling merrily. "You've gotta admit, it's been awhile."

Beth caught herself reflecting his grin right back at him. "Only twenty-odd years," she crowed. "Heck, I've barely had time to turn around and here you are again, just like that summer . . . "

"Yes, just like that summer." His face was thoughtful.

Silence surrounded them. Even the birds seemed to be intensely waiting.

In the heightened atmosphere, Beth could feel each ray of sunshine on her skin; she could hear each leaf that floated, soft as a raindrop, to the forest floor. It was like suspended animation, this feeling.

John simply stood there. He'd begun to suspect it was Beth in the cabin. He and Turk had spent the entire night watching, making certain nothing, or no one, came snooping back around. But until now, he hadn't been sure it was her, or that she was alone.

He glanced down at her hand stroking Turk's rough head. He wasn't really surprised that Turk had taken to her so readily. She had quite a way with animals, as he recalled. They'd saved more than one baby bird and at least one injured squirrel that infamous summer.

"And your dad?" he asked at last.

Tears welled but did not overflow. "Lost him two months ago," she whispered. "Cancer."

John frowned. "I'm very sorry, I thought I would, I mean I hoped I would, you know, get to see him again. I really thought a lot of that man."

"Thanks," she said. "I know he thought a lot of you, too." She sniffled and dug for a tissue in her pocket. Turk looked into her face, concerned. "It's okay," she told the big Shepherd. "I'm all right." Then, she sat on the nearest stump and wrapped her arms around Turk's neck.

John wanted to slip an arm around her, pull her head onto his chest, cry right along with her, but he had to remind himself that they weren't kids anymore; in fact, he didn't really know this woman at all. He'd known a young girl, years ago. But that was then, as they say.

He crouched on his heels a few feet away, hands dangling loosely between his knees, at a loss for words.

Beth wiped her nose, hoping against hope that it wasn't getting all red and stuffy.

They sat quietly for a moment, watching the sky darken above the pines. Beth untied her jacket from around her waist and stuck her arms in the sleeves. "Getting chilly," they both said at once.

She stood and John pulled the jacket onto her shoulders. His hands grasped the tops of her arms as he settled the jacket about her securely. Without a word, he turned her like a slow-motion top. Face to face, he knew she was the one he'd been looking for all these years.

Beth met his gaze and her dream came back to her in a rush. She thought she should pull away, she couldn't believe this was her old friend, the one she'd searched for over the years. "Still can't believe it's you," she said, reaching out as if to touch his face, but not quite touching it after all.

"And I can't believe you ruined a perfectly good guard dog," he replied tenderly, the kiss—if indeed that's what he'd intended—delayed good-naturedly.

Beth laughed. "And it only took a couple of hot dogs and some gentle persuasion." She rolled her eyes and smiled. "Okay, half a dozen hot dogs, actually."

John looked puzzled.

"He's visited me at the cabin a time or two," Beth explained.

Still shaking his head, John said, "I've seen him rip the arms off guys my size without a second thought. I don't get it, I just don't get it."

"Believe me," Beth replied, paraphrasing her father, "there are so many things we don't get." She paused, "I'm discovering more and more of them everyday." She thought about the colorful little lights, the text messages, Heaven. She sighed, wondering what he would think if she told him everything.

Walking back to her cabin, the silence was thick with unspoken questions and shared memories. The ground was squelchy beneath their feet. The pine needles created the best, the springiest, carpet in nature. In her mind, Beth recalled the shy, lanky boy, tanned beyond belief from never wearing anything more than cutoffs, the boy who had grabbed her hands and hoisted her up onto the gigantic boulder at the southern end of Stutter Creek. It was their special place, the one with the worn rope swing, the only spot where there was a pool deep enough for real diving and swimming.

It was on that boulder that they would stand, swaying and laughing, daring the other to jump first into the clear, freezing mountain water. It was there that they also shared picnic lunches and talked over the world's problems. It was there that he had confessed his feelings of loneliness, his feelings of never fitting in, of being on the outside looking in.

She, in turn, confessed how she felt like she should miss her mother, especially when holidays came around or when they made Mother's day cards in school or had Muffins for Mom days, things like that, but how her dad had always filled in so readily, never missing any of her events, so jovial and fun to be around... that some of her girlfriends were actually jealous of her. And it was the same with John, for even though they often felt as if they were totally on their own in the forest, they never really were; her dad was usually upstream fishing, or downstream urging them on, or better yet, right there beside them, jumping into the freezing water first.

They had been quite a trio that summer. Between Beth and her father, the two of them had unwittingly shown John what he had been missing in the way of family.

They walked on in comfortable silence for a while longer. It was as though the years had melted magically away.

At last, Beth asked, "Have you always lived here?" She hesitated, and then continued bravely, "What I mean is . . . I've been to your cabin. I peeked in windows. You weren't there. It looked like it was deserted."

John stopped in his tracks. "You—you were looking for me?"

"Of course." She wondered how much to divulge. "Every summer I would drag Dad up the mountain to see if you had returned." She looked into his face for confirmation that it was okay to go on. "You disappeared, John."

It was a moment before he spoke. "I guess I did." He seemed truly perplexed. "I never thought of it that way. I mean, I never thought I'd be missed."

"Where were you?" she asked.

"Did you marry?" he asked.

Speaking at the same time, they laughed self-consciously. Around them, the woods clicked and rustled back to life. Overhead, the swaying pines soughed gently in the slight breeze. Nearby, a squirrel chattered and then disappeared into a dark spot high up in the fork of limbs.

When they reached her cabin, they sat on the porch and she told him an abbreviated version of her life. She described, in loving detail, her daughter and new son-in-law. She also told him about the wonderful relationship her dad had enjoyed with Abby, the wonderful camping trips and sports activities, how she and her dad had delighted in showing Abby all their favorite places in and around Stutter Creek; and then her voice faltered.

"I'm not hearing much about Abby's father," John prodded, eyes kind.

Haltingly, Beth gave him the story on her marriage to Sam. With a hitch in her voice, she admitted how he had let her down, and how it had made her feel. "I never really doubted myself before, you know? Now, well . . ." She let the fall of her hair hide the rising heat in her cheeks. She wished she hadn't said that. It was too close to the bone. She'd never even admitted those feelings to Cindy.

John felt anger rising in his chest. How could anyone be so cruel to someone they were supposed to love?

Beth shook her head. "I thought he was a good man. How could I have been so wrong?" She glanced at John's face. "I thought we were in the home stretch." She laughed bitterly. "I was actually looking forward to early retirement. I thought I would be working on that novel I've been toying with for so long."

John was quiet, unnerved. In his mind, he had prepared himself to accept that she was a married woman, not a divorcee. He just couldn't fathom anyone voluntarily giving up on a relationship with the woman he had fantasized about for so long.

"Maybe it was just me, or something I did." Beth's expression was thoughtful. "You know, he never really understood my desire to write. When I won contests for fiction back in college, he always patted me on the back and then encouraged me to finish my teaching degree. Just like a parent, you know. Something to fall back on." She took a deep breath. "But he wasn't anything like my dad. I think he might even have been a little jealous . . . although I didn't find that out until we divorced. But he was a very good father to Abby, up until—oh never mind. I can't believe I'm telling you this. After all this time, what must you be thinking?" She was obviously flustered, embarrassed by her intimacy.

He was quiet for so long that Beth began to think all kinds of awful things. The porch felt suddenly small, cloying. Crickets chirruped; the shadows lengthened. It had been so many years. She didn't really know him. How could she have blurted out her entire sordid story? Such an idiot!

Finally, John stretched his long legs and leaned toward her conspiratorially. "Sounds like a real ass. Want me to make him disappear? I can do that you know."

Beth gasped. Then she realized he was only joking. "Only if you guarantee it will be slow and extremely painful," she replied.

He guffawed.

She was thankful that he didn't push her for details or offer false sympathy for something she really shouldn't have blurted out so readily. Encouraged, she changed the topic: "But what about you? Have you got someone up there at the cabin wondering what is taking you so long?"

John looked away. Now it was his turn to feel embarrassed. Dare he tell her why he had never married? Not yet, his common sense whispered; she's been through so much, no need to add to the burden. "No wife, no partner at all," he said. "Just me and Turk." He turned half toward her. "The job, you know; travelling the world. No time for romance . . ."

He was aware of how pompous he had sounded. "What I meant to say was that my years in the Army gave me a terminal case of wanderlust." He then offered her a simplistic version of what his career had entailed: early years in the Army learning how to defend both himself and others, going into private security, working for different multi-billion dollar companies always operating in war-torn countries. Constantly moving around, socking his money away, and eventually, dreaming of the little cabin in the woods. "When Turk was injured, something just hit me. I know he's just a dog—"

"Don't listen, Turk," Beth covered his furry ears with her hands.

"—but for some reason, the look in his eyes, the way he needed me that day. It made me realize it could just as easily have been me." His voice faded. "Except there would've been no one to look after me. To worry about me while I healed." He looked at her then. "No one but Turk." He slapped both palms down on his thighs. "That's it. That's my life." He shrugged and held out his hands as if to indicate there was no more left to say.

Beth nodded, shocked and surprised that there wasn't a wife or a special someone in his life. Not even an ex-wife, apparently. Was he being truthful? Or had she hit a nerve, asking about his romantic life? "So now you're retired?"

"Yep," he was obviously relieved when she didn't question his marital status further. "Looking forward to fixing up the cabin, planting a little vegetable garden . . . just breathing easy for awhile."

Beth nodded. "Sounds like a good plan." She ran her hands down Turk's back and shoulders. "But someday I want to hear the whole story of these awful scars." She felt very forward saying that, like she was forcing him to come back again, like a second date or something.

"How about tomorrow?" he suggested. "I think we've actually got a lot of catching up to do."

Unable to speak, all Beth could do was bob her head up and down like a chick pecking for grain.

"A picnic," John continued, standing. "I'll be here before lunch. Got a new ice chest and a brand new bill of groceries; bound to be some picnic stuff in there somewhere." He hesitated. "You do still like to hike, don't you?"

More head bobbing. "Yes, of course." Her breath was so shallow her voice cracked. "What do I need to do?"

"Not one thing." He laughed. "Let me handle everything." He leaned down and kissed the top of her head as though she were still a little girl.

He wanted to do more; he was so thrilled to find her there, he wanted to scoop her up in his arms and whirl madly around and around in a circle the way they had done that summer, holding hands and whirling like idiots to see who would get drunk and fall over first, laughing and throwing leaves and twigs at each other in mad made-up-on-the-spur-of-the-moment games of crazy tag—if I hit you with anything at all, you're it! They had really brought out the kid in each other, no doubt about it. Yet the news of her father's death hit him hard. The man should have had twenty or thirty more years. Suddenly it occurred to John that, in the back of his mind, he had always considered Beth and her dad to be kind of like his defacto family.

But the question was . . . did she feel the same? He was amazed to hear that she had continued to look for him. Why had he never considered the possibility that she might feel the same way he did when she got older? *Because I never had anyone to confide in. Because I never felt worthy of a family like that. Always assumed I was some kind of weirdo falling for a young girl like that.* But now, four years age difference was nothing. And look at all the years that had gone by . . . nope, best not to look. Besides, things always happen for a reason. Come to think of it, that had been her dad's philosophy. And John had taken it to heart all those years ago. He certainly wasn't going to start doubting it now.

With his head clouding with possibilities, senses on overload, John turned, and with a short whistle to Turk, was gone.

Beth floated through the cabin door as if in a dream. Had his lips lingered on her hair? She thought they had. She thought about pinching herself, but that seemed ridiculous. It was John. It really was. He even seemed the same as when they were teens. Was that possible? Look how much I've changed, she thought. Deep down, I'm still the same old me. But the exterior . . .

She ran both hands through her hair and walked into the bathroom to examine her reflection in the mirror. She felt self-aware for the first time in months, as though she had found a part of herself that had been missing. But were these just "rebound" feelings? Sam had hurt her so badly. What if John wasn't what he seemed either? Her mind wanted to pursue that avenue but her heart did not: I won't spoil it yet, she thought, not yet. See where it goes, see where this path leads.

She plopped down on the bed and sent Abby a long, rambling text message. She didn't have any idea when, or if, it would go through, but she had to tell someone how alive she felt. She was careful not to mention how she had longed for and searched for John during her teen years; she simply told her daughter that she had met up with an old friend and things felt brighter than they had in months.

Chapter Nineteen

Allie hugged her aunt and practically danced out to the car. Now that she had a plan, she was really looking forward to an afternoon of shopping, then maybe some pizza, or even a movie. She was so excited. When she had relayed the idea to Ginger, it had been all systems go.

She hurried to the car. In her mind, she was already trying on bathing suits and shorts. The Chevy Lumina was nice and warm after sitting in the sun all morning. Once inside, Allie started the engine, clipped on her seat belt, turned down the volume on the radio—why did it always seem so much louder when you got back in the car than when you got out?—slid her shades up on her nose, and backed out.

She was only about a mile out of town when he spoke.

"Pull over." His voice was rough.

Allie's eyes immediately sought the rearview mirror. She was horrified to see the disheveled countenance of the man she'd seen studying the Missing Poster this morning. Her first thought was that today would have been a good day to start locking the car—even if no one else in Stutter Creek did. The second thought was, is this some kind of a prank? She immediately thought of Ginger. Was this one of Ginger's friends from college or something?

"I said pull off the road you stupid bitch!" The voice was guttural, like a dull, serrated knife. Without another word, he slapped a length of Danny's cord around her neck and yanked backward.

In the time it took her to register that it was not a joke, Allie was inhaling what seemed to be her last breath. Her feet kicked out reflexively as her hands left the steering wheel and flew to her throat, fingernails digging into her own flesh as she fought to get a grip on the thin nylon cord cutting off her air. Just as it seemed she was destined to lose the battle, her right foot shot forward and smashed down on the accelerator. The instant acceleration caused Kurt to fall backward, jerking the cord even tighter.

Allie's world was almost completely black when she suddenly had the presence of mind to let off the gas and crush both feet down on the brake. Forward momentum abruptly halted, Allie's seat belt locked across her chest like a monstrous, rib-breaking hug. Kurt, teetering on the edge of the backseat, flew through the air past her head and smashed into the windshield. The safety glass cracked but did not break.

None of this registered on Allie's oxygen deprived brain. Her body was in pure survival mode. Adrenalin pulsed through her veins with each terrified hammer-blow of her heart. All she could think of was getting rid of the thing cutting into her throat.

Her clawing fingers finally grasped the cord that had been pulled from Kurt's hand. She whipped it off her neck, giving herself a stinging friction burn, but she didn't feel it. She could breathe again! Yanking the seatbelt buckle loose, Allie was out and running before she even realized she'd opened the door. Her mind was a blank white page. Her only thought: live!

Kurt sat up and shook his head. He had been temporarily stunned, but everything was coming back to him now. She was getting away. The little blonde slut, number three on his list, was getting away. He couldn't believe it. The first two victims had been so easy. Now this, on top of the fiasco with the woman in the Camaro . . . what had happened to Fate?

He slid beneath the steering wheel and took aim at the fleeing girl. "It ain't going down like this," he muttered, stepping on the gas.

Behind her, Allie heard the sound of her Uncle's old Chevy. Her fight or flight instinct was not over, not by a long shot. Without even thinking, running completely on reflex, she veered off the road and into the forest, her fists pumping, long legs skimming fallen logs and small deadfalls. She knew these woods fairly well. In the time she'd been staying with her aunt and uncle, she and her friends had roamed them freely. Two miles from here was the lake where they roasted marshmallows and played chicken in the water; a few miles past there was Ginger's parent's house. But before that, there was a cave. She and Ginger had explored it more than once with Ginger's dad.

Kurt drove along the road watching her carefully, looking for an opening. Shouldn't have varied the plan, he thought. This is what happens when you just react to circumstance instead of following the plan. He had intended to lure Allie to the side of the road on her way home from work in the evening using Danny, just like the others. But Danny was useless now. He couldn't even stand up.

Truthfully, he had been so intrigued by the idea of taking the girl in broad daylight, right out from under the Missing Girl poster, that he just hadn't been able to pass it up. Seeing evidence of his handiwork displayed in public like that had excited him tremendously. He'd gotten cocky again. Just like with the woman in the Camaro. He'd actually attributed the coincidence of seeing the drugstore girl park the unlocked car behind the drugstore to Fate, again. Big mistake. Now look what had happened.

Suddenly, he gunned the engine directly toward the spot where he could see her disappearing ponytail flipping like the flag on a white tail deer. Up into the edge of the forest he flew, stomping on the brake at the last second as he plowed up an incline directly between two massive pines. Shoving the lever into park, he flung himself from the car. She wasn't getting away. Fate or not, she was his.

Allie didn't slow when she heard the car leave the road. She was headed up the mountain. One part of her mind screamed that it was suicide trying to outrun the killer going uphill, but she was positive she could make it to the hidden entrance of the cave. Only locals knew about it. She would be safe there. If she could just make it to the cave, she was pretty sure she would be safe.

Kurt couldn't believe it; the girl was heading straight for his hideaway. He slowed to let her think she was getting away. Fate? She was going exactly where he wanted her. He felt inside his pocket to make sure he hadn't lost the duct tape during the struggle in the car.

***

John gathered the supplies for a picnic and stashed them in the new Coleman ice chest on wheels. It really wouldn't be much of a picnic; he had invented the idea on the spur of the moment to give himself a good excuse to be around her cabin early the next morning. In truth, he and Turk intended to spend the night there, again. He added his camouflage sleeping bag to the small pile of picnic supplies. Last night, sitting with his back against a tree for hours, had been uncomfortable. He wasn't a young man, not any more. He laughed, thinking of how the years had passed so quickly, and then he turned his mind back to the present.

His night goggles—the ones with infrared—went into the bag. He wouldn't carry his gun; he was afraid he would use it too readily. His trigger finger was way too itchy for civilian life, yet. Better to leave it behind and avoid the possibility of "jumping the gun" so to speak.

After sundown, he and Turk would set up a quiet, smokeless camp just west of her cabin. From that angle, John thought he could see both the front and back of the house at the same time. The creek bordered the east side of the property. He thought it unlikely anyone would come from that direction.

For a moment, he regretted not telling Beth that someone had been hanging around. It would be better if she were on her guard, but after all she'd been through, he didn't want to mar their reunion with his paranoia. He was sure that's all it was. After spending the last twenty years on constant guard, he was finding it next to impossible to turn off his reflexes now. Most likely the person who had been near the cabin last night was just some camper from the other side of the mountain who didn't realize he was on private property.

***

By the time Ray got Janie back to the top of the ravine, a trucker was just pulling off the road to see if he could help with the flat on the Mustang.

As Ray told him the about the dead girl in the ravine, Janie clung to him like a near-drowning victim who'd just been pulled from the ocean. He felt it very likely that she was going into shock.

Spitting his ever-present toothpick onto the ground, the trucker's eyes—his name was Dax—grew wider and wider as Ray told their story.

"And ya'll just happened to be out walking down there," he indicated the bar ditch with a jerk of his head, "after leaving your car, with the engine running, and a flat tire?"

Even through his own shock, Ray could hear the skepticism in the man's voice. He was sure he would have felt the same way if the roles had been reversed.

"It was sort of a spat," Ray tried to explain. "Jane jumped out of the car in a huff and I just took off after her." He realized that now he was saying that he had chased one young woman into the same place where another young woman lay dead. "But the woman, er woman's body, isn't in the bar ditch, it's in a ravine on the other side of the ditch." He shook his head as he realized he wasn't helping his cause at all. "Actually, it sounds a lot worse than it is."

"Hell!" Dax interjected. "Don't know how it could sound much worse. Dead body sounds pretty damn bad no matter how you tell it!" He began to back toward his truck. "Maybe you know how that gal wound up in that ditch," he said softly, never taking his eyes off Ray. "Might be you planned on leaving that one down there, too." His face clouded noticeably. "You got her drugged or something?"

Ray looked at Janie. She was barely staying upright. If he hadn't been clasping her firmly about the waist, she would probably be lying in a boneless heap at his feet. He shook his head, not believing the way things were getting turned around. "She's the one who found . . . the body. It was horrible." His eyes strayed involuntarily toward the ravine. "I think she might be going into shock." He jiggled Janie's chin with his free hand. "Wake up!" He said. "Tell this guy what happened!"

Janie's head bobbled; her eyes rolled. A teardrop shaped globule of saliva slipped from the corner of her mouth. Both men watched as it hit the shoulder of the road. It made a faint dark spot in the dust.

"I'd been teasing her when we had the flat," Ray began to babble. "And she got out and took off walking. She walked right off in the ditch." He wiped the back of his hand across his mouth as if the spit had been his, not Janie's. He glanced at the trucker imploringly. "I swear it's the truth . . . I don't know anything about that—that other girl." And then a thought occurred out of the blue. "Have you got a blanket?" he asked.

Dax was momentarily dumbfounded. A blanket? What'd he want with a blanket? Maybe to wrap up the body? Then it hit him: shock. The young girl was shivering and drooling. Maybe she really was in shock, but he didn't want to take his eyes off the boy—he looked kind of like your run-of-the-mill hoodlum—long enough to get a blanket. Then an idea hit him. "If you're on the up and up," he said. "Then gimme the girl and go get the keys out of your car so I'll know you ain't gonna run off the second I turn my back." He realized that he might be giving the guy an opportunity to escape, but as long as he had the girl, Dax didn't care. She reminded him of his own daughter back when she'd been that age.

Ray nodded and shuffled over to where Dax was standing. He noticed the cell phone he was holding.

"I dialed 911," he said. "Law oughtta be here soon." He glanced at the tire iron mounted on the backside of the cab. It was the one he used to thump the tires each time he started a new trip.

Ray noticed him looking at the tire iron, but he wasn't worried about that. He was just glad the guy was finally taking him seriously.

He pictured his own phone tucked into the console of the Mustang.

Dax slipped his arm around Janie's waist. He did his best not to touch Ray or let Ray touch him. Ray thought, I could really give him a heart attack right now if I suddenly yelled Boo! But of course, he didn't. It was just his wild streak again—the one that had gotten them in that ravine in the first place. Maybe his dad was right; maybe it was time to grow up.

Without further ado, Ray hurried over, turned off the Mustang, grabbed his phone, and rushed back to hand the keys to Dax.

"Sorry, man," Dax said. "I just couldn't take a chance on you being, you know, something other than what you say." He shifted Janie carefully to his other arm and then opened the door to the sleeper cab on his truck. "Think I ought to put her in here? Or just wrap her up and put her in your car?"

"Let's just wrap her up and put her in the Mustang," Ray said. "She might freak out if we tried to hoist her into the sleeper. You say the cops are on the way?" He absolutely hated being out of control like this. He wondered if that is why Janie got mad so quickly. Maybe she felt out of control when he was joking and throwing his weight around like an idiot. Like he could do whatever he wanted.

"Cops are on the way," Dax replied, handing Ray an orange and white blanket. Together they wrapped it around Janie and placed her gently in the passenger seat of the car. She looked at Ray and he thought he saw a gleam of recognition in her eyes. "Wish we had some coffee or something to give her. Even a drink of water, anything. I just want to do something—hey, are they bringing an ambulance for the, you know, body?"

Dax shrugged. "I got a bottle of water in the truck. I don't know about an ambulance." He looked up. "I called when I saw you leading her out of the ditch. I didn't know about the body." His eyes still registered a hint of suspicion. "Guess we're about to find out. Here's the Brewer County Deputy now."

Rookie detective, Woody James, took the call from the Brewer County Sheriff's Department. Even though Amanda was found in Brewer County, and she'd gone missing in Carrel County, the Attempt to Locate had covered the entire state.

"Sounds like our girl." He hung up the phone. "Officer described a young blonde who appears to have been raped and strangled. Not necessarily in that order." He shook his head. "Certainly fits the description of both Amanda and our suspect's modus operandi."

Senior Detective Kendra Dean was already pulling on her jacket. "I'll drive," she said.

Chapter Twenty

Kurt saw Allie just inside the cave's almost-hidden entrance. She had stopped in her tracks when she spied Danny lying in a heap, hands and feet tied so that he couldn't move, much less walk. He didn't appear to be breathing.

Allie was bending down to get a closer look when Kurt crept up behind her and delivered a double-fisted hammer blow to the back of her neck just at the base of her skull. Administered just right, such a blow could cause instant loss of consciousness. Just another neat trick he'd picked up while incarcerated. His lawyer had advised him to use his time in prison to further his education; now he was infinitely thankful that he had followed that advice.

As soon as she went down, Kurt slapped the duct tape over her mouth and began to drag her toward the rear of the cave. The old woman would have to wait. When he was finished with Allie, she was going into the abyss. He couldn't wait to hear her body hit the bottom of the seemingly bottomless pit. Too bad the daylight didn't reach back there; he could only imagine what she would look like lying way down at the bottom of the shaft like a discarded rag doll. That would be an image he could take on the road to examine again and again. It would keep him warm on those cold, cold nights.

He rolled her over on the damp cave floor and jerked down the zipper on his stolen jeans even as his other hand began squeezing her windpipe.

Shoving his pants off his bony hips, still smashing down on Allie's throat with all his weight, Kurt straddled her and tried to yank her shorts off with his free hand. In his excitement, he forgot to undo the buttons. He became enraged, taking his hand from her throat to tear at the fabric as if he would rip it from her body.

Allie's stunned brain awoke. She pulled her knees up and instinctively began to rock from side to side, trying to free her body from the hateful burden.

Cursing, he reached for her throat with both hands.

But Allie was still in survival mode.

She whipped her head from side to side.

She couldn't dislodge him, but she was able to prevent him from getting a death grip again. On instinct, she reached between his legs and grabbed his scrotum. With both hands she twisted and squeezed and dug her nails in with all her remaining strength. She heard and felt something rip and then warmth began to trickle into her palms. Blood, she thought. I hope that's blood.

Kurt tumbled over, moaning and holding his crotch.

Allie jumped up, and ran straight off the edge of the world.

She had escaped her predator only to fall right into the deep shaft at the back of the cave. She didn't make a sound.

Kurt could not believe his luck had run out. He screamed in pain and anger, but no matter how he tried, he could not see down into the pit. It was solid black. He cursed himself for not buying more flashlight batteries; his had run out after only a few hours.

Falling back on his heels, Kurt examined himself. He was still in great pain, but he wasn't throwing up, so he took that to mean he would survive. The blood had stopped, too. Apparently, she had only torn the skin with her nails.

He pulled the jeans back on with a grimace of pain. Now he was more determined than ever to take care of the bitch down in the cabin and move on. Everything had been going according to plan until she entered the picture. She was like an albatross; he had to get rid of her and get on with things. It seemed as though fate had deserted him, and he was sick of this place and everything in it. All he wanted was to get out, and get wasted. But first, he had to get rid of the woman in the cabin.

Now, it was personal.

He glanced at Danny lying in the corner. The kid was dead, or at least as close as anyone on this side of the dirt could get. Pitch him in the abyss with the girl?

Kurt couldn't decide. He had intended to do just that, but not yet. He'd really wanted to use Danny to lure the old woman up here and then pitch them both into the abyss—but was it really wise to leave his son with the victims? Wasn't that sort of like saying Okay, Feds, I did it. Come and get me . . . Not that he expected them to ever be found, not if the abyss was as deep as it seemed. But still, there was no sense in being foolhardy.

Technically, of course, he didn't kill Allie. She ran off into the shaft on her own—okay, she did it to get away from him—not exactly the same, but no judge would see it that way. She was his victim no doubt about it—and he hadn't even gotten to enjoy the fruits of his labor.

That really pissed him off. It wasn't fair. He'd gone to all the trouble to get her up here, and then wham! She was gone, just like that.

He was determined to wrap things up and have some fun before returning to his list. He grabbed another stout length of cord from his backpack and started off down the mountain, limping slightly. By the time he made it back down, it would be near dusk, the perfect time to grab an old woman who would not be expecting him.

He checked his pocket for the tape, took it out, tore off several six-inch lengths and stuck them on the sleeve of his jacket as he walked. The nylon cord would have to be cut with a kitchen knife after he'd bound her hands behind her back. He'd used the shorter one on Allie. Now, it was lost.

Kurt's new plan was already taking shape in his twisted mind: retrieve Allie's car—in his excitement, he'd almost forgotten about it—drive it to the old broad's cabin, and ask her nicely to accompany him to his "campsite" to check on the boy. If she refused, he would simply force his way in, slap the duct tape over her mouth, tie her hands, and then march her up the mountain to the cave where he could have his fun—if he was even still able after what the blonde had done. Then, he would let her join Allie in the pit. He still wanted to use Danny to lure the prosecutor to her doom, but that was looking like a pipe dream now. On the other hand, there were many, many children out there, unattended. What worked once would probably work again.

But ... first things first. When the albatross was gone, he would carry or drag Danny's body back to the girl's old Chevy. Somewhere down the road, in another state, the car would have to burn. That should take care of the boy and the evidence. Tossing him into the pit with the women was too risky. The two women probably wouldn't be found for weeks, maybe even months. Maybe never. But when they were, if his boy was with them, he knew the Feds wouldn't stop until they caught him.

He just hoped no one had noticed Allie's car. Since she was a local, he needed to get it off the road, fast.

Slipping and sliding, he hurried back down the mountain, eyes roving from side to side, watching for the spot where he had chased Allie into the trees.

When he saw it, he began to whistle Brahms Lullaby again. Her car was almost as well hidden as if he'd planned it. Jammed in between two trees some distance off the road, only the tire marks looked suspicious. But apparently no one had been suspicious enough to check. Things were going to work out after all. He pulled his work gloves back on and tried to ignore the fiery pain between his legs. Sweat from his slip-sliding trek back down the mountain was stinging the deep gouges in his groin.

He extracted one of the mementos from his pocket and licked it. The simple act helped him refocus. He was still furious at Allie for scratching him and then committing suicide, depriving him of his fun and messing up his plan, but it was going to be okay. The old woman in the cabin was going to take her place.

Making certain no cars were coming from either direction, Kurt stepped into the Chevy Lumina as if he owned it. The engine had died, but the keys on the pewter angel key ring, which read *Never drive faster than your guardian angel can fly,* were still in the ignition. It turned over sluggishly when Kurt tried it. It seemed as if he'd been gone for hours, but it had actually been only minutes. Dust that had been churned up when he plowed off-road still floated through the slanted rays of late afternoon light. The old car appeared to be coated with a fine layer of 14-carat dust.

He backed carefully out of the trees and executed a sloppy three-point turnabout on the narrow country road. Deep pools of pine-shadow leaked across the road at every turn trying their best to drown the single-lane in darkness.

Soon, he would be at the old broad's cabin. He began to whistle again. The thought of her on her knees made him smile. It made him feel powerful.

***

Beth stood on the front porch watching the sun set over the creek. It looked like a painting the way the last rays of light lay like a wrinkled swath of gold down the middle of the stuttering creek. Hummingbirds flitted in and out of the porch overhang, gathering sustenance from the two feeders she had hung only yesterday. The little birds acted as if they'd just been waiting for her to return and feed them.

The way they buzzed around her head reminded her of her father's colored lights. A trio of the flying jewels buzzed past her face, close enough to make her flinch. The twilight was very quiet. Beth felt her flesh prickle, as if someone had caressed her with a feather. She clasped her elbows and rubbed at the skin until the feeling returned to normal. A gentle breeze brought her the tang of damp pine. She thought of John and Turk preparing a picnic for tomorrow, and the thought made her feel hopeful for the first time in a long time.

She wanted to stay on the porch a while longer, the air was as silky as a set of good sheets, but a mosquito broke the silence directly beside her ear and she swatted at it, remembering that her can of bug repellent was inside on the kitchen counter. As she turned to pull open the screen door, she heard a car pull into the circle drive.

John, she thought, one hand going automatically to her hair to smooth and pat. He must've come back in his car. Maybe he was thinking of her, too. She took a deep breath, preparing her face to be pleasant but not elated. Inside, she was actually thrilled that he hadn't been able to stay away.

She began to turn around, the careful smile on her face, and that's when she was hit.

He plowed into her without a word. Beth had a brief glimpse of filthy brown hair and some kind of hunter's jacket with lots of pockets, and then she was on her knees inside the cabin, duct tape covering her mouth and a terrifying maniac smashing her to the floor from behind.

The fiend had crashed into her, without slowing, knocking her over the threshold. She tried to scream, to cry out for John or Turk, or even her father, but the tape was snug against her skin. She tried rubbing saliva around with her tongue to loosen the adhesive, but it didn't work.

Suddenly, she had no more time to worry about her mouth; now he was dragging her arms behind her, one knee in the small of her back, holding her down, wrapping her wrists with cord. *How could this happen right inside my own front door?* "Dad!" she screamed soundlessly. "Help me!"

Kurt was taking no chances. When he'd seen her standing there, alone, he'd forgotten all about his plan to ask her to accompany him. The urge to overpower her was irresistible.

"Stop struggling!" he hissed, jerking her up by her elbows. "That kid you saw was mine." He knew she would understand what he was talking about. "Come with me, or he dies!" Pulling her along by her "leash," Kurt rummaged through the drawer holding the kitchen flatware, searching for something.

Beth tried to twist her head around to look at him. He was looking for a knife to kill her; she knew that's what he was doing. She thought of the kitchen scissors tucked into the "catch-all" drawer opposite the sink. Could she reach them, like this, with her hands tied together? She had to try. She was not going anywhere without a fight. If only John and Turk were still around—John was twice the size of this creep. Suddenly, the image of the girl on the Missing Poster flashed through her mind and she understood that this monster was probably the kidnapper.

What she didn't understand was why he said the boy was his, or why he wanted her. She thought killers and kidnappers usually stuck with a type of victim. I'm not young or blonde, she thought. Why me? But clarity wasn't forthcoming because he had finally found a knife and was sawing away at the nylon cord that he'd used to tie her hands. Apparently, it was much too long. He cut off several feet of the cord and stuck it in one of his many pockets.

Beth worried about his plans for that extra cord. I've got to watch for a chance to run. I've got to be ready. Then he was pushing her from behind, and it was all she could do to scramble out the back door and off the porch without losing her footing and going down on her knees again.

"Move!" He shoved her again, prodding her with the point of one of her very own steak knives.

The fact that he wasn't taking her to the car really worried her. She was certain he was going to kill her in the forest and bury her in a shallow grave—one he had probably already dug. What about the boy?

Feet slipping on the tricky carpet of pine needles, tripping over exposed roots and downed branches, Beth tried to think of a way out, a way to get loose. But with him pushing her, and her only source of air coming through her nose, the going was rough and getting rougher. She was in fairly good shape, but she was no teenager. Fortunately, the trail was slightly luminescent in the good light of the rising moon. Oh Dad, she thought again, where are you—please help me—please!

Halfway up the mountain, Beth felt her captor turn loose of her right elbow to swat at something buzzing around his face. She thought she caught a glimpse of color from the corner of her eye, but it was hard to tell. Droplets of sweat were collecting in her hairline, plastering her hair to her forehead. It was all she could do to stay on her feet;

she didn't dare glance up for more than a second for fear of falling over something. The woods she loved so much had suddenly turned traitor. Nothing was familiar and everything seemed like a prop from a slasher flick. The higher they went, the darker it got. Once, Beth was positive she saw an old white car camouflaged by pine braches. It was at the very end of an unused trail. Whoever had driven a car up that trail was asking for trouble, she thought. Then she realized it probably belonged to the monster behind her—or even to his victim.

She kept thinking she might wake up. This scenario would certainly fall right in line with one of her nightmares . . . but then the madman would poke her between the shoulder blades or in the small of her back and she would realize she'd begun to lag. She would try to pick up the pace for a few steps, but in the darkening woods, it was like being blind—or at least playing blind the way she and her friends had done as kids—close your eyes and try to walk through the house or across the yard without killing yourself. She used to love that game. But this was no game, and no dream, either.

Suddenly he stumbled and fell into her. "Pick up your fucking feet!" he demanded, pushing her so hard she fell to one knee.

And then they were there. The new moonlight showed a slice of blacker darkness that Beth realized must be the opening to Blue Cave. She'd forgotten all about it. She hadn't been near it since she was a teen up here with her dad.

Dodging a face-height tree branch, she tried to remember how large the opening was. But Kurt pushed her when she balked, and then the branch was the least of her worries for suddenly she was falling with no hands to catch herself.

Beth didn't see what she'd tripped over, but she was pretty sure it was human, it was warm and the surface gave to the pressure of her Reebok's when she inadvertently kicked it as she stumbled. Even terrified as she was, Beth wondered why the form didn't grunt or cry out when she'd kicked it. In her gut, she was certain it was the boy. Was he dead?

She felt her fear ratchet up another notch. Her breath tore at her throat, and the air coming in through her nostrils was damp and fetid. She tried to be as quiet as possible, hoping the killer was as blind as she was inside this horrible blackness.

Chapter Twenty-One

Ginger was embarrassed when the waitress came by for the third time and asked if she was ready to order yet. She'd tried Allie's cell phone, but not surprisingly, there was no signal. The mountains were notorious for blocking reception. In fact, it was more unusual to get a signal than not get one.

Finally, after half an hour, she gave up and ordered a Personal Pan Pizza, pepperoni with mushrooms. She requested another Diet Coke in a to-go cup she could take with her. A couple of rhinestone cowboys were giving her the eye. One had already offered to fill in for whoever had stood her up.

The fun had gone out of the evening. She was just ready to get out of there and find out why Allie really had stood her up. Probably that Jurassic Chevy she insists on driving, Ginger thought. Maybe I'll just head toward Stutter Creek and see if she is stranded somewhere. Better call her aunt first, though.

She begged an area-wide phone book from the greasy kid behind the counter and looked up Martha and Joe's home number. She knew they closed the drugstore around five or six depending on the number of customers, but she seldom had reason to call them on their home phone.

When the phone rang, Martha and Joe were sitting in their easy chairs in front of the TV. They had just eaten the soup which she'd brought home from the drugstore, and she had taken her shoes off and propped her chronically aching feet on the embroidered hassock.

Heaving her tired body up from the chair, wondering who could possibly be calling that she hadn't just talked to at the drugstore, Martha's intuition kicked into overdrive and she began to mentally list the whereabouts of her closest friends and relatives. Allie was the only one out of pocket. She cursed her creaky old legs and tingling toes, but she made it to the phone on the fifth ring.

"Never got there you say?" Martha repeated after Ginger told her why she was calling. Then she clutched the clunky old-fashioned receiver to her chest and fainted dead away onto the braided country-blue rug.

As she came around, she saw Joe struggling to get up from his recliner dragging his oxygen canister behind him like one of Little Bo Peep's sheep. "Don't look at me like that," she said. "I'm all right. Just talk to Ginger on the phone." She sat up on the rug and held out the receiver that she still clutched to her chest.

As soon as Ginger repeated her reason for calling, Joe realized why his wife had fainted; she'd brought home one of the Missing Girl posters in order to show him the resemblance to their beloved Allie.

Jose wasted no time in calling the Stutter Creek Police chief at home. The chief was one of his and Martha's oldest friends. Not only had they graduated from the same high school together back in '56 (along with the twelve other students that had made up their senior class), but Chief Brown also ate breakfast, lunch, and dinner at the drugstore almost every day. He'd lost his own wife of forty-five years to heart disease just last year. He said he was too old to learn how to cook.

Martha watched as Joe dialed Chief Brown's number. It was a testament to her faith in her husband that she sat absolutely silent while he relayed the story to his friend. Not once did she try to interrupt.

When Joe hung up the phone, he held his hands out to his wife. She knew he didn't have the strength to help her up off the floor, but she took one of his big paws anyway, and then pushed herself up on the edge of the antique telephone stand with her other hand.

As soon as she gained her feet, Martha burst into tears and buried her face in Joe's white-t-shirted chest. This was the worst thing that could've happened.

This is it, she thought. This is it. But even through her tears she was already cataloging what she needed to tell Roger Brown. What had Allie been wearing? What were her exact plans? When had she left the drugstore? What was the license plate on the car?

She settled Joe back in his recliner, and then slipped the stub of a pencil out of her apron pocket. She hadn't even changed out of her work clothes yet. On the back of an order pad, Martha began to write down everything she could think of that might help the Chief find her niece. She hesitated when she felt Joe's eyes boring into her face. "What?" she looked at him.

His face was heavy, as if in the last few minutes he had actually gained weight, and that new weight was dragging the flesh of his face down into a scowl. "You know what we have to do," he said.

For a second, Martha was completely at a loss. Wasn't she making a list already? Then it hit her. They had to call Allie's parents and tell them their only daughter was missing and she just happened to be the spitting image of another girl who had been lost for days.

Feeling the pencil slip from her grip, Martha pulled her apron up and hid her face again. She didn't think she could handle this after all.

Even though he felt powerless, Joe picked up the phone, but instead of his younger sister's number, his fingers automatically dialed Allie's cell phone. Just let me make sure. Then, if there's no answer, I'll call Angie.

Allie's phone went straight to voice mail. Just like it always did when the mountains interfered with reception, he thought. Just like always. But without hesitation, he went ahead and dialed his sister's cell phone. She was a dark haired copy of Allie. She, too, had boundless energy and a happy outlook. It was a good thing she did. Allie had come along very late in her parents' life. They had completely given up on having children when they got the wonderful surprise.

Joe caught Angie at the gym. She often stopped there on her way home from her "sit-down" job at the bank. "Where's Greg?" Joe asked when she picked up.

"Still at work, I think." Her voice belied her puzzlement. "Do you need to talk to him?"

Joe nodded silently. Should have called him in the first place, he thought. I can't tell my baby sister that her only child is missing, and then expect her to be able to drive herself home. "Yes, it's Greg I needed to speak with," he lied. "Got a construction question. I just dialed you out of habit. Talk to you later." He hung up feeling like the world's biggest coward. Then he dialed Angie's husband's number.

Greg picked up immediately. Joe had a feeling Angie had beat him to the punch, was on the other line perhaps, so he got right to the point. "Can you go to Angie's gym right away?" he asked.

Greg sounded like he was already shoving things in his briefcase. "Of course," he said. Joe knew they figured something was up. "What is it, Joe?"

Hearing the jingle of keys and then the ding-ding-ding of the alarm as Greg opened his car door and climbed inside, Joe crossed himself, he was a lapsed Catholic but in times of stress the old habits came out of hiding automatically, and prayed that he wasn't jumping the gun and worrying them needlessly. Then he realized what he was thinking. He changed his silent prayer: he prayed that he WAS worrying them needlessly.

Wiping his forehead, he said, "It's Allie, Greg . . . she left here on her way to meet Ginger in Pine River for pizza, but she never arrived."

"What?" Greg sounded confused. "Is she okay? Where is she?"

Joe's old heart thumped crazily, boosted by the panic he heard in his brother-in-law's voice. "We haven't heard from her, she didn't show up at the pizza place. I'm sure she's okay." *Why did I say that*, he wondered. "I've alerted the Police so they can begin to search her route."

"Dear God . . ." Greg exhaled audibly. "How long has she been gone?"

Glancing at the old Regulator clock on the dining room wall, Joe replied, "Been about an hour since she was supposed to have met Ginger. Been gone over three hours, all together. Had the afternoon off."

Silence for a moment, then Greg replied, "Well, okay. That's not so long." His voice was somewhat shaky. It was obvious he was comforting himself to keep the panic at bay. "Probably just had a flat or overheated radiator or something. Might even be walking back as we speak."

"You're probably right," Joe agreed. "Us old folks probably just jumped the gun." He couldn't bring himself to tell Greg about the Missing Girl poster. "I just thought you both should know, but I didn't want to tell Angela without you there. Will you tell her right away?"

"I'm on my way to pick her up. Did you . . . I mean, I suppose you tried Allie's cell?"

"Yes. But you know how these mountains are . . ."

Greg acknowledged that the mountains were probably the cause of the problem. Then he agreed to call Joe as soon as he and Angie got home. He didn't want to tell her until they were together. Then they would leave her car at home and drive straight to Stutter Creek in his.

Chief Brown hadn't changed out of his work clothes, either. All he'd done was place his service revolver, holster and all, on top of the refrigerator and pour himself a glass of iced tea to go with the sandwich Martha had put in a to-go box at the Drugstore less than an hour earlier. He had been one of the last customers of the day.

Before he even put his belt back on, he went to his cruiser and pulled one of the Missing posters off his clipboard. The Pine River PD was listed as the contact agency.

When he dialed the number and identified himself, the dispatcher patched him straight through to Kendra Dean's mobile phone.

After perfunctory introductions—they'd actually met at a conference a few months earlier—Roger Brown outlined the problem.

Detective Dean realized the implications right away. "Could be our guy. Too close to home to be otherwise; also the same victim type: young, blonde, and predictable. Too many coincidences. Besides, better safe than sorry, I always say. Especially where serial killers are concerned." Her voice had taken on a confidential note. "We found the body of Amanda Myers late last night. Waiting on forensics to verify the ID, but I know it's her. Can't put it on the wire until proper identification, of course, and the family notified . . . but I'm telling you. Go ahead and drive your girl's route and begin the search. We'll be there in half an hour to give you our information and assistance."

"Any suspects yet?" Brown asked.

"Got some DNA . . . semen, saliva, running it through the system now. Bastard hasn't given us any prints yet. Good gloves, I guess."

"How about a profile?" Chief Brown asked.

"Not yet," she admitted. "Why? You got an idea?"

Brown sucked in his gut as he buckled his seat belt. "Got a new guy in town. Hermit type, cabin up on the mountain. Lived here a while when he was a kid, been gone twenty, maybe thirty years." He was picturing John as he spoke. "Great big guy; talked to him once at the post office; said he'd been working overseas. Worth checking out, I guess. Seemed a little shy, like I said, but he certainly seems to be making his home here. Keeps to himself . . . I don't know."

"Definitely worth talking to," Dean agreed. "Be there shortly. We'll pick him up together." She clicked off without further ado.

Chief Brown headed to the drugstore. He wanted to drive the exact same route that Allie would have driven. He called Joe and Martha and found out that Allie had mentioned going to Miller's Outlet before she left town. He called dispatch and got George Miller's home number from the key card file. Every business in town was listed in the key card file, along with at-home numbers and other emergency numbers in case the Fire Department or Police Department ever needed a key to the business. "Roger?" Mr. Miller's was obviously concerned. "Something wrong at the shop?"

Chief Brown cleared his throat. "Not at all, George. I'm calling to check on Allie, Joe and Martha's niece. Martha said she was going to stop by your place on her way out of town." He hesitated to let the information sink in. "She was going to meet a friend in Pine River. But she hasn't reached her destination, and we can't raise her on her phone."

"Hmm." George Miller stroked his chin thoughtfully. He confirmed that Allie had made several purchases that afternoon, but he couldn't remember exactly when. "Gracie," he called over his shoulder. "Do you recall what time Allie was in the store today? Or more precisely, what time she left?"

His wife, whose name was really Deidre, but whom he had called Gracie since the day they met. "I think it was around three, maybe three-thirty," she said. "Is something wrong?"

Roger Brown could hear the concern in Deidre Miller's voice even though she wasn't actually talking to him. "Here's the problem," he said, and then he told them everything. He believed the more people in on a problem, the quicker the likelihood of a solution. Besides, these people were his friends, both the Millers and Joe and Martha. That was the best and the worst thing about being the Police Chief of a small town: he knew all the locals.

Every one of them.

Chapter Twenty-Two

Kami and Corey Jesson picked up her mother and left Sunset headed for Pine River where the body of a young woman lay waiting for them in the city morgue. Kami knew it was her sister. She felt it inside, in the pit of her belly, in the marrow of her bones. She thought her mom was holding onto hope, but even though Kami did not know what to expect, she felt sure there was no hope.

Corey said he would go in and make the identification if they would let him, but Kami said she would do it. In spite of all their fights and petty jealousies growing up, Amanda was her only sister, her only sibling. She would go in, with or without her mother, alone or with Corey, it didn't really matter. Right now, she only knew that the most important moment of her life was just around the corner, and she was not going to screw it up.

She was trying to put things right by proving that no matter how horrible the image, how nightmarishly unforgettable, she would carry it with her for the rest of her life as an homage to what Amanda had suffered. In that small way, she felt she was honoring her sister, saying, "I'm sorry Sis; I would have been there if I could."

***

It was Chief Brown, driving the route from Miller's Outpost, straight though town to the single lane black-top, shining his spotlight the whole way, terrifying deer and rabbits galore, who first saw the tale-tell marks where Joe's Chevy Lumina had left the roadway and plowed up the earth as it skidded to a stop amongst the spiky pines.

"I'll be damned." Fear gripped his gut as he stepped from his cruiser, careful not to tread on the fresh tire tracks.

Aiming the spotlight at the greatest area of chewed up earth, Brown pulled his heavy-duty flashlight and walked a little further into the trees. He could hear his own breathing. It was very loud.

"Out of the car near the third forest entrance," he said softly into the radio mic clipped to the shoulder of his uniform.

"10-4," the dispatcher responded. "Backup?"

"10-40, please," Chief Brown responded conversationally. That meant yes, send the back-up unit quietly, no lights, no sirens.

The dispatcher clicked the mic switch once to acknowledge the end of the exchange. From this moment forward, all other radio transmission would be kept to a bare minimum in order to give this situation their full attention. They didn't have much excitement in the small town, but the Chief insisted they keep up their training. They were often called upon to assist the DPS or the Sheriff's Office out on the highway or on those lonely country roads. They took their jobs very seriously.

Chief Brown knew something had occurred here. He and his officers were on this road several times every day. It was the main route to and from Pine River, the nearest large town. If the ugly gash had been there very long, one of them would have noticed it.

He continued to shine his flashlight in a circular pattern as he walked slowly around his patrol car. Then he saw the footprints. He wasn't a tracker like his Native American friend, Hully, but any fool could see that someone was running and another someone was chasing. He felt certain Allie was the prey. One set of prints was small and light; the other set was a bit larger and much deeper.

Pulling a handkerchief from his hip pocket, the Chief wiped his face and took a couple of deep breaths to calm his adrenalin-fueled nerves. This felt bad. He could easily picture sweet little Allie running for her life. He remembered her grin this morning as she served him his eggs and bacon. She was as guileless as a newborn lamb.

He drew another breath, exhaled, hitched up his utility belt, and continued. He thought he could follow the prints with his flashlight. They appeared to be on a very specific diagonal path going always upward toward the top of the mountain.

"Following tracks," he said into the mic. "Eric, you in route?"

Officer Eric Hagar replied. "ETA 2 minutes."

"I'm on foot going northeast away from my cruiser. You'll see my light."

Officer Hagar clicked the mic.

As long as the footprints continue, Brown thought, Allie's alive. He kept that thought in his head as he plugged slowly on, up and up the mountain. "Dispatch," he spoke again. "Advise Detective Dean of my location."

"10-4," the dispatcher replied.

Moments later, following the directions from the dispatcher, Detectives Dean and James approached the possible crime scene silently. The identity of their victim had been confirmed. Both were contemplating the possibility of another. Neither had the slightest doubt that a serial killer was in their territory.

Suddenly, Dean braked and yanked off her seat belt. "In the trees, your side," she barked. "See him?"

"Got 'im," Woody James said as he unholstered his weapon. "Halt!" He commanded, leaping from the vehicle. "Sheriff's Office!"

John stopped in his tracks. He and Turk had gotten almost to the trail leading to Beth's cabin. He'd seen the marked vehicle, but since there were no lights or sirens, he'd assumed they were just passing through on their way to somewhere else. He was glad he'd left his own gun at home.

"On your knees. Hands behind your head," James demanded. Then he glanced at Turk. "And make sure your dog is under control. I don't want to have to shoot him."

John nodded curtly at Turk.

The big dog sank to his belly. Neither he, nor his master, had uttered a sound. John realized something was definitely amiss in the forest. The S.O. didn't normally approach people by telling them to get on their knees. He felt the first fingers of dread clutch at his heart. Not for himself but for Beth. They weren't close enough to see the cabin yet, but the very fact that they were in the area made him think something was wrong.

The woman detective appraised the situation.

"I appreciate your cooperation. And his." She nodded toward Turk.

"Got any ID?" she asked matter of factly.

John nodded looking at her badge. "Front jacket pocket." He knew better than to retrieve it himself. "Driver's license. Security ID, retired."

"Former military?" Dean asked.

John nodded again. "Many years ago."

Dean pulled the cards carefully from John's pocket, never letting her gaze slip from his face.

John could sense her nerves humming. The eye of the other officer's Glock never left his forehead. He knew that the slightest wrong move on his part would result in his or Turk's death. Maybe both. He prayed they would hurry. He wanted to check on Beth. He couldn't bear the thought that he had just found her and now she might be in trouble.

"You're the new guy in Stutter Creek, aren't you?" Dean asked, examining his ID with a penlight clasped in her teeth. "Chief Brown said you're renovating a cabin at the crest . . . "

John kept his cool. "Yes. Recently retired. Came home."

"Why are you skulking around in your camouflage tonight?" James demanded.

"Friend lives in that cabin down the hill." He indicated the direction even though the cabin was barely visible. "She's seen odd tracks, heard something near her place the last couple nights. I was checking it out." He wanted to shift his position. Although he could kneel here for hours if need be, he wasn't sure his patience would hold out that long. Everything in the forest had gone unnaturally quiet. Even the breeze had stopped moving.

"Sir Lancelot," James said sarcastically, pulling a pair of handcuffs from his belt. "Maybe we'd better put you in the car. We're going to meet up with Chief Brown right now. Maybe you should be there, too."

John didn't want to leave without checking on Beth, especially now that he knew the detectives from Pine River were meeting up with the Police Chief of Stutter Creek. It meant something was definitely going on. "I'm not sure why you are taking me into custody like this," he began as James put the cuffs on his hands. "But apparently you are here for a reason, so could we at least check my friend's cabin to make certain she's okay? Then I'll go with you and do whatever you want me to do."

Dean heard the sincerity in his voice. "You say it's close by?"

"Just at the base of the mountain." He indicated the direction with his head again. "Her driveway intersects the road you're on."

Dean nodded and they loaded both John and Turk into the backseat of their car. She radioed the dispatcher and had her relay their situation to Chief Brown. He asked whose cabin they were going to, and when John said Beth's name, he told the dispatcher to let him know the outcome immediately. He and his officer were still tracking, but it was slow going as they often had to backtrack and restart when they lost the tracks in loose piles of leaves and pine needles. They also had to be extra careful not to walk on the tracks themselves.

John asked where the Chief was, but he really didn't think they would tell him. But Dean must have decided he wasn't as big a threat as they'd led on, so she told him what was going on.

When John learned that a girl's body had been found and that a local girl was missing and possibly being tracked up the mountain, he became agitated as they rounded the curve and saw the two vehicles in Beth's drive.

"The Camaro belongs to Beth," John volunteered. "I think I've seen the Lumina parked outside the drugstore in Stutter Creek. I think the owner's niece drives it."

The two detectives looked at each other. "She's the one who's missing," Dean said, cutting her lights and slipping the gearshift into park.

Drawing her weapon, Dean nodded at Woody James and they clicked their door handles almost simultaneously, in the quietest manner possible. There were no lights visible inside the cabin.

"You can't leave us in here," John rasped. "If Beth is in there, she might be hurt. If she isn't in there, Turk can track her . . . please. Let us help." His voice broke.

"Sorry," Dean said. "You were in the area. I don't know you, and I don't know what's going on here. Sit tight, we'll be right back."

Woody James nodded his agreement and they eased their doors the rest of the way open.

In that instant, John also made a split-second decision. "Turk!" he commanded. "Find the woman!" Then he jerked his head toward the half-open passenger-side door. He ducked as the huge Shepherd shot over the seat, clearing the doorframe and knocking Woody James to the ground as he crashed into the backs of his knees.

"Don't shoot!" Dean yelled as James, on his belly, trained his sights on the hindquarters of the disappearing canine.

"Wish you hadn't done that," she said to John. "If the dog gets in the Chief's way on that mountain, he'll shoot first and ask questions later. At least I know I would."

"Beth isn't in that cabin. She wouldn't be sitting in the dark. Besides, if she was in there, Turk would have gone in. He wouldn't have passed it by."

Detective James was dusting himself off. "So you think he's actually tracking her?"

John nodded. "I know he is."

"Let's check the cabin," Dean said. "No more shenanigans from you." She pointed her chin at John. Then she radioed dispatch again, and told them about the situation with Turk. She did it more to protect the Chief and his officer than to protect the dog. He was huge. If he came lunging out of the forest near the officers, there was no telling who might get shot.

John had taken their measure. He knew now that if he did decide to escape, they would not shoot him in the back. He would wait to see what they found inside Beth's cabin before he acted; but if things didn't seem right, he'd already decided he would kick out the window and follow Turk. He could think of no reason the missing girl's car should be at Beth's cabin if Beth wasn't there. And it had been barely an hour since he had been here himself. Beth had not mentioned having plans with the young woman who was now listed as missing. And then there was that episode when Turk had alerted near the cabin for seemingly no reason.

The lead detective approached the front door while the junior detective slipped around behind.

John watched anxiously.

Suddenly, lights blazed inside the cabin and he could see their silhouettes searching from room to room. Then they were back.

"Signs of a struggle," Dean said. "Small amount of blood on the floor, back door screen was sprung and hanging open."

"Someone took her up the mountain," James added. "And we know it wasn't you; footprints were far too small."

John sat up straighter. He had been in a half-crouch, ready to launch himself out the window if necessary. "Take these cuffs off and let's get after Turk."

"How will we track him?" Detective James asked as he removed the handcuffs.

John pulled a slim silver dog whistle from his pocket. "He'll come and get us." He blew into the mouthpiece silently.

Chapter Twenty-Three

Beth fought her rising panic. Where was he? What was he doing? She sat as still as possible, hoping the kidnapper couldn't hear her heart pounding inside the cage of her ribs.

The silence was a weight; it pressed against her skin as surely as if she'd been fathoms deep in the ocean. In fact, somewhere she could hear the faint drip, drip, drip of water and while she was concentrating on its location, he found her.

He loomed out of the darkness like the shadow from her nightmare, pushing her over onto her back, grinding her still-bound hands and arms into the rough surface of the cave floor. Rocks and sharp pieces of shale cut into her flesh, and all she could hear was his harsh breathing as he struggled to remove her jeans.

She kicked and fought more wildly than even she would've have believed possible. Until he hit her.

It was a hard, glancing blow to her nose and cheek that brought tears to her eyes and clogged her nose with bloody mucus. He ripped at her with the steak knife, attempting to cut off her clothes, slicing her skin along with the fabric.

She cried a muffled cry and thrashed and twisted and kicked until, somehow, the knife skittered away across the floor. It was so dark she couldn't see him until he came at her again. This time he grappled with her until he found her neck, digging in with his fingers, squeezing and squeezing, hanging on as she thrashed and kicked.

And between his hands, the tape on her mouth, and the bloody mucus clogging her nose, Beth couldn't breathe at all.

Her movements grew weaker . . .

But still, there were thrashing sounds.

It was a great tremendous thrashing and crashing that she knew at once had to be Turk charging up the mountain, tearing through the underbrush toward the cave just as he had charged at her in her own driveway.

In her mind she cried out to him and to John and to her father but mostly to God. *Please God let him get here in time.*

The man let out a string of disbelieving curses under his breath as the noise grew closer and closer. His fingers loosened and she could hear him scuttling toward the entrance to see what was coming.

She rolled over onto her knees, gasping for air, and pressed her back into the cave wall, somehow managing to gain her feet. Her jeans were halfway down her legs and she scraped them down with her feet and said a silent thank you when she was able to kick them away without falling. She gagged and swallowed the bloody mucus clogging the back of her throat, but more took its place.

Any moment, she thought. Turk will rush through the entrance at any moment. She held her breath and listened . . . the crashing sounds were growing fainter. He was going the wrong direction. It sounded as if he was going back down.

She hung her head. She prayed that her dizziness was the reason she couldn't hear the dog anymore—but no time to wonder.

The maniac was coming at her again. This time she was on her feet and she lashed out at him with a sideways kick as soon as her peripheral vision told her he was within range. Suddenly, Beth realized that her dad's colored lights were swirling about the cave, lighting the man's silhouette each time he got close to her.

She heard growling coming from somewhere and for a moment she was sure that Turk had returned. But it wasn't Turk. It was her. The growling was coming from beneath the tape still covering her mouth.

***

When Detective James freed him, John blew the silent whistle and then took off up the mountain trail at a dead run. The handcuffs still dangled from one wrist. He would worry about that later. Already he could sense that Turk was returning. It wasn't that he could hear him from that distance; it was that he could sense a shift in the air that separated them. His lug-soled boots dug into the springy earth, and he was certain he could feel the earth pushing back, spurring him on.

In his mind, Detective Woody James was thinking, praying, that he hadn't just released a killer. The big man had taken off as if he'd been shot from a circus cannon. The detective had the feeling there would be no slowing him either, short of a well-placed bullet. What if he and the small man were accomplices? Neither of them had mentioned the fact that there were two vehicles but only one set of footprints that could've belonged to a lightweight woman. Could the killer be a woman? What if the heavier set of prints belonged to the woman in the cabin, and the lighter set belonged to the girl? So many possibilities. His first big case, and he may have just released the killer.

"It's not him," Detective Dean said, as if she could read his mind—when in reality—she probably could read his face. "Serial killers don't usually have trained dogs." She scowled. "Not that polite, anyhow."

They continued up the mountain cautiously, hands on their weapons.

Chief Brown knew Blue Cave was nearby. He just couldn't find the entrance in the darkness. In fact, he had gone too far. Both he and Officer Hagar were now above the cave and they had lost the tracks.

They headed back down slowly; their feet occasionally slipping and sliding in the mucky patches of half-melted snow and wet leaves. It was a lot trickier going downhill.

They stopped abruptly when they heard Turk crashing through the underbrush. Chief Brown assumed it was a buck or maybe even a bear just out of hibernation. He and Hagar pulled their weapons at the same time.

The chief motioned the officer behind him. He shined the flashlight toward the sound, but then the noise stopped and began to move away back down the mountain.

Both men exhaled shakily.

The chief began to wonder if searching in the darkness was wise. Then he imagined Allie's face, and he knew the search would go on. Just have to be even more careful, he thought, as he holstered his pistol. That's when the dispatcher relayed the message from the detective about Turk.

"That animal we heard must've been him," Chief Brown whispered. "Glad I didn't shoot."

Halfway up the trail, John stopped, too. He was listening to the forest. And he was waiting for Turk to find him. In a matter of moments, the big dog was there. This time they both headed up the pitch-dark trail, swiftly and silently. John kept his hand on Turk's collar so they wouldn't get separated.

Inside the cave, Kurt pulled the remaining length of cord from his coat pocket and stretched it between his hands like a garrote. The knife he'd taken from the cabin was gone. He'd been unable to locate it in the darkness.

It didn't matter. He intended to finish the job right now. He crept toward the wall where the woman was cowering. Those damn fireflies had followed him into the cave. He'd never seen anything like it—they seemed to glow with all the colors of a Christmas tree. Must be hallucinating, he thought.

Certainly wouldn't be the first time; maybe it was an acid flashback or something. Nevertheless, he swatted at them as if they really were multicolored insects.

Beth thought she could outsmart the man with her dad's help. Since she could see the colored lights around him, she thought she could make it to the entrance and slip outside to hide in the brush. She was almost certain Turk had been looking for her. If she could stay hidden from the kidnapper long enough, she was sure the big dog would find her.

Carefully, even more quietly than the dripping of moisture off the cave's ceiling, Beth eased her feet across the floor until she was crouching right next to the lighter shade of darkness that signified the cave's opening. She could feel a cold draft coming through from outside. From out of the silence, she heard a soft moan. Perhaps the boy was alive after all. She had to go. She had to get help for herself and for him.

Inhaling as deeply and quietly as her clogged nose would allow, Beth stepped through the opening and into the night. She was no longer thinking, now she was just doing. Without another moment's thought, she slid through the draft and was gone.

Kurt was right behind her. He had realized what she was doing, but when Danny moaned, Kurt had hesitated, and that hesitation afforded her the fraction of a second she needed to disappear.

Desperately, Kurt flipped the noose of cord sideways and downward just past the last place he had seen her crouched outside the cave.

Beth gagged as the cord skimmed over her face like a lethal thread thrown by a giant spider. She tried to jerk free, but that made it worse. Kurt yanked upward with both hands and Beth's world fell away. Colored lights were everywhere, in her eyes, in her head, in the air around her. She couldn't breathe at all. He had won.

Suddenly Turk exploded from his master's grasp and launched himself up the remaining thirty feet of ground. In three gigantic leaps, he crashed solidly into the man like a fur-covered freight train. One hundred fifty pounds of teeth and muscle took him down. The impact was accompanied by a nightmare of guttural snarling, gnashing, and crushing. It sounded as if the guy's flesh was being ripped straight off the bone.

Powerful flashlights lit up the scene as a scream of agony split the night like an axe splitting dry wood. The screaming went on and on as Turk dragged the bad guy around the clearing by his forearm. He was waiting on that one word from John that would okay the kill.

Beth lurched forward into the thorny brush as the cord fell harmlessly away from her throat. She sucked in as much precious air as her nostrils would allow, but her vision was still iffy. This time the spots in front of her eyes had nothing to do with her father; they were purely from lack of oxygen.

Over the sounds of the melee, a man's voice could be heard shouting, "Call off your dog before he kills the guy!"

Beth wanted to say, "No! Don't you dare call off the dog." But she couldn't say anything, her mouth was still covered with filthy dirt and leaf encrusted tape.

The Chief was right, John knew he couldn't risk having Turk put down simply for doing his job. This wasn't Kazakhstan. With a sharp command he instructed the dog to "drop and release." Turk let go and dropped to the ground.

The man rolled to his feet dripping blood and cradling one crushed and mangled arm in the crook of the other. He raced directly between the two men, the Chief, who had come hurrying upon the scene from above the cave, and John, who had come upon the scene from below the cave. Neither man had yet seen Beth lying in the brush. But just when the kidnapper appeared to be about to vanish into the trees, John snagged his jacket.

The forward motion pulled them both off balance and down they went.

Suddenly they were upside down rolling head over feet down the mountain. Somehow John grasped the short chain that had been connecting the handcuffs on his wrists and now it was cutting right into the kidnapper's windpipe, one end still fastened around John's big wrist, the other securely grasped inside his opposite fist. Together, they rolled over and over and over down the steep trail until they came to a violent stop in a stand of slender saplings. There was no fight left in the twisted little man.

He was dead.

Detective Woody James found them just as John disentangled himself from the suspect. The young detective did not know what to say or where to start. He put two fingers to the suspect's neck, checking for a pulse, but he found nothing. When the senior detective caught up, Detective James was just unlocking his bloody cuffs from John's wrist. The big man explained what had happened.

Kendra Dean nodded. "Saved the taxpayers the trouble and expense of a trial." The she indicated the cuffs. "Those will go into an evidence bag."

Detective James pulled clear plastic gloves and a brown paper bag from a pouch on his belt.

"Beth?" John gasped, head down, heaving.

But neither detective knew where she was. Then Turk was beside him and he simply allowed the dog to lead him back up the trail to where Beth lay, still bound, valiantly attempting to pry the tape off her mouth by grinding her face into the wet earth.

John knelt beside her and gently helped her stand.

Jerking her head from side to side, she let him know that the tape on her mouth had to come off first.

Chief Brown was there with his flashlight. He'd already alerted dispatch for an ambulance and the Medical Examiner, and as soon as one side of the tape was peeled up, Beth cried, "There's a boy in there. I think he's still alive!"

The Chief started toward the cave. "What about Allie?"

Beth yanked her head sharply. The remainder of the tape ripped away taking a layer of skin off her bottom lip. "What do you mean?" she asked, tasting blood. "What about Allie?"

"They think he may have taken her," John explained, indicating the crumpled figure lying halfway down the slope.

Beth followed his glance. "Is he dead?" Her voice was rough.

John nodded. He, too, was covered in dirt, scratches, and damp leafy debris. But his calloused fingers were working deftly at the knot binding her wrists together. "Did you see the girl, Allie?" The knot came free and he pulled her to his chest as she grimaced at the pins and needles flooding her hands. Rubbing them gently, John continued, "Her car was at your cabin when we got there."

Beth shook her head, confused. "That can't be. She wasn't there."

Then the Chief was shouting for someone to come and help him with the boy. "He's barely breathing. Eric, tell that ambulance to hurry!"

The two detectives rushed to the cave to lend their flashlights to the darkness. The Chief had already pulled his utility knife and cut the cords tying the boy's feet and hands together.

Suddenly, massive barking from the rear of the cave ricocheted off the walls as Turk alerted his master to the location of someone else.

John and Beth rushed inside, and, with the aid of Woody James, shined the police issued megawatts down into the abyss.

"Help," a tiny voice cried. "Please!"

Allie was crammed onto a jagged ledge ten feet below the lip of the shaft. The beams of the flashlights reflected dully off the remains of the silver tape still tangled in her blonde hair. She had spent the last couple of hours wondering if the sounds above her were real or if they were in her head. She'd banged it pretty hard when she leapt.

Later, she told them that she'd remembered the shelf when she jumped up to run away from her captor, but she hadn't known if she could land on it, or if she would just career off and crash all the way to the bottom. "I took a chance," she told them later. "I knew I was going to die anyway." They were all amazed at her bravery and her presence of mind. Her ability to keep her wits about her had undoubtedly saved her life.

With gear from Chief Brown's patrol car, John and Woody James were able to fashion a rope "chair" for Allie to sit in while they carefully hoisted her to the surface. She looked a lot worse than she sounded. But of course she hadn't had the chance to tell them about the struggle in the car and the horrible sprint up the mountain. Chief Brown and Officer Hagar already knew about that, though. Those were the tracks they had been following all along.

Allie collapsed shortly after they pulled her up. The way she was bent over in pain, John was pretty sure she had some broken ribs. He just hoped they hadn't punctured a lung or worse. He'd once seen a shard of rib bone driven right through a victim's pericardium and into the heart itself. Allie's left wrist was obviously fractured, and her head, well, if she didn't have a concussion he'd be surprised. She was so cold that he suspected she might also be hypothermic.

But the boy . . . it was nothing short of a miracle that he was alive at all. He was a skin-covered skeleton. Even he couldn't remember the last time he'd actually had a meal. A hamburger he said, but then he retracted that memory when he further recalled that Kurt—whom he insisted was really his father, for pity's sake—had thrown it out the window when he'd complained that it was gritty. He'd had some beef jerky, he thought. But he just wasn't certain. By the time the paramedics loaded him onto the stretcher, he was unconscious again. He'd slipped away as soon as they started trying to insert the intravenous line into his poor, dehydrated arm. The pediatrician at the E.R. radioed that they should quit messing around and get to the hospital as quickly as possible.

Beth was strong. Other than some balm for her bleeding lip and the numerous cuts, scrapes, and superficial knife wounds, all she wanted from the paramedics was something to ease the rope burn across her throat.

Allie had that same thin line across her throat, too.

"Karma," John said when he saw the marks on the women. "He's sporting his own jewelry, now." Secretly, he thought it very fitting that he had accidentally killed the guy in the same manner that he had attempted to kill the two women. Later, he would learn that Kurt's first two victims had sported strangulation "necklaces," too. Only their marks were bruises, and they had not lived to tell about it.

Chief Brown insisted on following the ambulance carrying Allie and the boy to the hospital in Stutter Creek. He made John, Beth, and Turk ride with him. Once in the car, he immediately instructed the dispatcher to notify Joe and Martha to meet them at the hospital. They, in turn, called Greg and Angie who were just getting into town. Angie then called Ginger and told her that Allie had been found alive.

Ginger said she would meet them at the hospital.

Officer Hagar was left to wait for the Medical Examiner. Detective James stayed with him. Detective Dean drove to the hospital to interview Beth and Allie for her report.

Allie was not able to answer any questions. In fact, once she was being cared for in the hospital, she went to sleep and did not wake up for two days.

The doctor in Pine River—where she was transferred when it was decided she needed to be near a neurosurgeon just in case the head trauma was worse than they thought— said it was most likely just her body's way of coping with the aftereffects of her ordeal.

Beth agreed to spend the night in the Stutter Creek hospital for observation, but she asked John to retrieve her purse and her cell phone from the cabin. She wanted to call Abby and Cindy and let them know everything was okay. She wasn't the least bit surprised to find both a text and a voice mail from Abby wanting to know what was wrong. Her daughter seemed to think she had been in danger.

"You must be psychic," Beth texted back. "I'm okay, but you were right, I was in danger." Immediately, the phone trilled.

It was Abby.

Beth couldn't help it; she sobbed out the whole sordid story. When she came to the part about her heroes Turk and John, Abby interrupted with a question of her own: "John . . . the childhood friend you ran into?"

Beth admitted that he was one and the same. Then she had to explain who Turk was and what part he played in the rescue. Finally, she took a deep breath and told Abby all about the colored lights and the text messages from her dad.

"Grampa texted you from the great beyond?"

Beth wasn't surprised at the skepticism she heard in her daughter's voice. "Not only that," she replied. "He saved my life by showing me where the killer was inside the cave."

"But I thought you said the dog saved you . . ."

Beth frowned. "That's true, even though I got outside with Dad's help, the maniac caught me again. That's when Turk arrived. But if Dad hadn't helped, I wouldn't have been out in the open at all. I probably would have been lying at the bottom of that shaft—it's hard to explain."

Beth figured that Abby wondered about her mental state, but Beth, of course, insisted that she was fine. "No, I don't need you to come home. You just barely got back to Rome. I'm fine, I promise! As a matter of fact, I'm just about to call Cindy and give her a report. And you know what? I think I'll make a trip to visit you and Terry before the summer is up. I've never been to Italy. Will you show me the sights?"

Laughing, Abby replied, "Of course, Mom. That would be wonderful. Thank God you're okay . . . and Mom?"

"Yes?"

"I do believe you about Grampa—after all, I knew the moment I woke up this morning that something was wrong. That's why I called—I knew in my heart that something wasn't right."

Beth sighed. "I'm glad you believe me. I just wish I could have told him thanks one more time."

"I'll bet he knows," Abby interrupted. "I'm sure he does."

Ending the conversation after promising to call again in the morning, Beth whispered, "Dad? You still around?"

The phone beeped softly indicating a new text.

I KNOW, the message read. I KNOW.

She saw a tiny flicker of color near the ceiling. "I love you, Daddy. You saved my life."

LOVE YOU TOO, BABY, ALWAYS AND FOREVER. I THINK I SEE YOUR MOM UP AHEAD—SHE LOOKS SO YOUNG. I'M LEAVING YOU WITH BIG JOHN NOW. THANK GOD YOU FOUND EACH OTHER AGAIN.

Beth's eyes filled with tears. "Tell Mom I love her."

The lights winked and disappeared. The phone beeped, but there were no more words.

Chapter Twenty-Four

Greg Moreland looked down at his precious daughter lying so still on the sterile white bed and he was reminded of a national news story a few years earlier about a pair of friends who were in a horrific car crash together. One lived and the other died immediately. But the one who lived was misidentified and so her parents thought she was dead. The parents of the dead girl thought she was the one alive and battling for life in the hospital. Greg couldn't remember how long it was before the poor disfigured girls were correctly identified, but looking down at Allie's bruised and swollen face and her lumpy, misshapen head, he could understand how it could happen. He'd seen the poster of the other missing girl. She was a carbon copy of his Allie, even down to the way they both wore their blonde hair.

Suddenly Greg was certain he was looking not at his little Allie, but at a stranger's daughter. Perhaps it was his little Allie who was lying dead on a cold pull out metal slab in the hospital morgue. Maybe she wasn't here at all. But wouldn't he know? He was certain if his precious girl had left this earth, he would know. Somehow.

Wouldn't he?

Furtively, he looked over his shoulder to see if anyone was watching, he had to know. Had to be positive. There was one thing he knew of that would convince him that this still pale form was truly his daughter. He carefully lifted the sheet on the left side of the young woman's body.

And there it was: the tattoo she thought no one knew about. It was a tiny tattoo of a crouching black panther located just above her left hip. It was her high school's mascot. He had a feeling it had been a graduation night dare. Her mom had caught a glimpse of it a few days afterward when she'd inadvertently walked in on Allie stepping out of the shower.

To his surprise, Angie had not thrown a wall-eyed fit; in fact, she had pretended she hadn't even seen it. She'd only mentioned it to Greg later that evening when they were getting ready for bed. He was doubly surprised that her tone had been calm and rather indulgent. Actually, they both knew that they had been very lucky where Allie was concerned. If one small tattoo was the worst of her rebellious phase, they could definitely live with that.

Now he was glad she had seen it because there it was, right where Angie had told him it was. It's funny how the most minor things often happen for a reason, he thought. He lowered the sheet carefully, his vision blurring unexpectedly at the proof. He hadn't realized how worried he was. Odd that no one had thought to mention it considering how unrecognizable she was, but then, they had found her car at that woman's cabin. This time, two plus two did equal four. Thank God. She really was a mirror image of the other girl. He prayed that her family would find some measure of peace. Though he couldn't imagine how he would have, had the roles been reversed.

Feeling a bit more hopeful, he allowed Angie to come in and sit while he headed to the cafeteria for a cup of coffee.

Amanda Myers's family intercepted him as they were coming up from the morgue. It was as if his worries had conjured them out of the air.

They passed each other in the corridor and then Kami stopped, excused herself from the others, and hurried after Greg. Touching his arm hesitantly, she said, "Excuse me, are you the other girl's father?"

Even deep in thought, Greg knew what she meant. "Yes. I'm Allie's dad. Her mom is sitting with her right now." He felt the need to explain why he wasn't with her. He wanted them to know she had not been left alone.

Kami cleared her throat. "I--I just . . . I don't know. I wanted to say I'm glad she is alive. Will she be okay? My sister was one of his victims; we just came from the morgue. We drove in from Sunset." She seemed to realize she was rambling as she half turned and indicated the rest of her family. Her husband was literally holding up his mother-in-law. Her face was soft and loose. She didn't even glance in their direction.

Greg wondered if the mom had been given a sedative or something. He felt incredibly guilty that his girl had survived and theirs had not. Yet, he was still so thankful. Impulsively, he enveloped Kami in a loose-armed bear hug.

She collapsed against him, sobbing.

Greg wondered if it was the first time she'd allowed herself to show her emotions. He could only imagine how horrible it must have been, seeing her sister's bruised face.

Guiding her to a small area of chairs, Greg nodded to her family that it was okay, and then he sat and held her while she railed against the madman that had taken Mandy's life.

Eventually, Kami's mother looked up and wandered over. She stood beside them for a moment, absently watching her remaining daughter sob on the shoulder of a stranger. Then she sat down beside her on the orange Naugahyde connect-a-chair and pulled Kami to her.

Greg got up and walked into the cafeteria as if in a dream. He was exhausted and empty. Eventually, he thought he would fill up that emptiness with even more gratitude; but right now, the thing he felt most was a cold conviction that the world was nothing like he had always believed. Evil, he thought. There really is a deadly evil that pulses just below the surface of our everyday lives.

***

At the Sheriff's Office, Janie's father had Ray backed into a corner. He was questioning him and reading him the riot act at the same time. All the while he was talking, he was inching closer and closer to the young man's face. Spittle was flying and his finger was itching to punctuate his words.

Finally, it did: "And I don't know what my daughter was doing in that ditch beside your car with a flat tire and no spare, but if you ever think about trying to contact her again, boy, you better think and think again!" That's when the hard stubby index finger poked Ray in the chest. Each time the man said the word think, that hard finger jabbed Ray just below his collarbone.

Ray's first instinct was to slug the old dude. He'd never been so disrespected in his entire life. However, maybe he had grown up a bit in the last few hours. He pushed away his instinct to lash out at the older man. Instead, he used his head. He decided if he ever wanted to see Janie again—and he most definitely did—then he was going to have to suck it up and grovel.

"You're absolutely right, sir," he began. "I was an idiot for not replacing my spare the last time I had a flat." He resisted the urge to rub the spot where the index finger had been poking. Instead, he continued, "Being a mechanic, I really have no excuse other than what I already said: I'm just an idiot." Ray looked down at his shoes, then, so the older man would not think he was being flippant because he wasn't. He really did regret the whole thing. Since the poor dead girl was beyond help, he wished with all his heart that someone else had found her. He was pretty sure the image of her lying there in the ditch would live in his head from now on. And he didn't even like to think of how many ways it might affect Janie. She was so young, and tenderhearted.

"Don't be too hard on the boy," the deputy said from across the room. "If not for them, we wouldn't have found that poor girl until the animals had pulled her to pieces just like the other one." He frowned. "That one still hasn't been identified. Don't know when she will be identified. At least this little girl's folks will know what happened to her. Must be awful not to ever know . . ."

Janie's father stepped away from Ray and sank down at an unused desk. "Just don't think you're ever going to take her out again," he said in Ray's general direction. "She sure as hell don't need some damned fool don't even know how to keep a car runnin'."

Ray glanced at the deputy and mouthed a silent "thanks."

The deputy nodded.

Janie was still in the ER with her mother. It looked like she was going to be admitted for observation. The ER doc said she would be all right after the shock wore off and she slept for a while.

Ray had already decided he was going to the hospital as soon as they were done taking his statement here. He didn't care what her father said. He'd be polite, but Janie would know he was there. He wouldn't let her down again.

Many years later, when Ray was actually his son-in-law, Janie's father would admit that he had focused on Ray that night because he felt so helpless at the hospital. Janie had been semi-conscious and he didn't know how to handle it. Therefore, he had taken it out on Ray. "You really did deserve it, though," he told him. "You were quite an idiot back then. It's a wonder I didn't just kill you and tell God you died."

By then Ray had gotten used to his father-in-law's sense of humor—and his John Wayne way of dealing with the world—and he simply replied, "Well, I'm glad you showed some self-restraint. Your grandkids thank you, too." And then he grinned because he knew he had been lucky and blessed in more ways than he could ever count. It was as if the act of finding Amanda's body had solidified something between him and Janie. Perhaps it had just made them both grow up.

It had taken months of sitting on Janie's sofa watching videos and playing Monopoly with the family before he was ever even allowed to be alone with her again, much less take her out on a "date." But Ray never regretted a moment of it. They had three wonderful children as proof. He did indeed open his own garage eventually, and Janie's little brother, Bill, who had once been something of a black sheep, became his right hand man, and his best mechanic.

Since her mother was in prison and no other relatives came forward, the remains of Sherylyn Combs were buried by the county after she was identified as being the victim whose arm had been found by Officer Lujan in the suburb of Yellow Bend. Her name had been first on the hand-written list they'd found in Kurt's jacket pocket. Ms. Candy Deevy and Ms. Shaniqua Patterson took up a collection at Wal-Mart and ordered a simple headstone for Sherylyn's grave. It helped assuage their feelings of guilt, somewhat.

Chapter Twenty-Five

Beth started dialing Cindy's number. She'd had a reply to her earlier text about meeting John and planning a picnic—a lifetime ago—but she was so exhausted and relieved to be lying safe and clean in this nice white bed, that she'd fallen sound asleep in the middle of dialing. Surprisingly, whether due to the drugs the doctor had ordered or simply due to fatigue, this time, her dreams were sweet. Perhaps it was simply because there were no more shadows in her life. They had all been banished.

Later, the light from the hallway dimmed considerably as the massive bulk of John Stockton filled the doorway. He stood quietly, watching her sleep. When he was certain her chest was indeed moving up and down, he crept in and placed a card and a perfect pink rose on the nightstand.

Turk was waiting in the truck. John had made a quick trip to The Corner Store where Juanita, having already heard about the heroics of her favorite canine, had picked out and gift-wrapped a special bison bone just for Turk. Juanita was the one person in Stutter Creek who was on more than a nodding acquaintance with John and his dog. Part owner in a small buffalo ranch in addition to The Corner Store, she'd been supplying them with bones and bison steaks since the day John had come in for his first it-feels-good-to-be-home bill of groceries.

In the truck, in the hospital parking lot, Turk was gnawing happily at his reward. The passenger side window was down, no danger of theft with Turk riding shotgun, and a cool breeze wafted through the cab, ruffling the thick fur around his neck. The clean scent of snow was still on the breeze, and if he could have spoken, Turk might have said that the scent of bison combined with the clean fresh breeze was just what he needed to get the stench of Kurt out of his snout.

It was near dawn the next morning when Beth awoke. A nurse's aide had opened the curtains, and the room was bright, but disappointment settled about her like a cloak when she realized she was alone. Of course, it was her own fault. She'd told Abby not to come—not that she could have made it from Europe in such a short amount of time anyway—and she had never even contacted Cindy.

Okay, admit it, she chastised herself. You expected John Stockton to be sleeping in that fold out recliner. He'd said he would be here, and even though you know how men are about vows and promises, you still expected that fairy-tale Prince Charming—

She spied the pink rose on the nightstand.

Wiping at a stray tear, she picked up the flower and the card. For several moments, she just lay with the two items balanced on her chest. She knew it was from John, and it made her very happy. On the other hand, they weren't kids anymore—what if he wasn't the same sweet guy he used to be? Did she really want to get on that roller coaster again? Did she really want to fall in love only to find out he wasn't what he seemed?

"I would be dead if not for John, and Turk," she said aloud. Her voice was raspy and her throat was sore, but that wasn't the cause of her consternation. Beth just wasn't sure she wanted to be indebted to someone for the rest of her life. Sam had not only pulled the rug out from under her emotionally, she felt as if he had set that rug on fire and burned it to a crisp then buried the ashes. And that was before the psychopath—

Idiot, she chided herself mentally. *You're alive. You've been given a second chance. Be thankful for that. It doesn't have to be anything more—even if the superhero was the hunky friend you searched for all those years.* She actually sighed when that thought slipped into her mind.

Then she laid the rose aside and opened the envelope containing the card. The front of the card was a sunrise over mountains; it was hand drawn and painted with watercolors. Inside, the card was blank except for three lines of calligraphy:

The picnic basket is packed.

Get well soon.

Love, John and . . .

She turned the card over and laughed out loud. A huge paw print took up the entire blank space.

When she looked up from the card, he was standing in the doorway. "I've been watching you sleep," he said. Then he held up the picnic basket. "I know it won't be today," he said. "But when you're ready . . ."

Beth grinned. "You've got a date. But first, tell me about Allie and the boy."

He sat down beside her on the bed and told her that Allie was expected to make a full recovery. Besides two cracked ribs and a broken cheekbone, the doctor suspected the concussion was her most serious injury and probably the reason she was still unconscious. They didn't consider it life threatening, however.

"They found a list in the pocket of that guy's jacket," John said. "Allie's name was #3 on the list." He hesitated as if gauging her response. "Apparently the remains of victims #1 and #2 have been found in, or near, Pine River. There were two other names on that list after Allie's."

Beth's face drained of color. She had almost convinced herself it had all been a bad dream; after all, she only had some minor cuts and abrasions. "Oh my God," she said. "Was my name on the list?"

John shook his head. "The detective seems to think you were just in the wrong place at the wrong time."

Nodding, she replied: "It all started when I saw the boy standing beside the road."

"His name is Danny," John said. Then he told her all the information Woody James had relayed about Danny's abduction and his use as bait. "They've even located the boy's maternal grandmother. Apparently she was in an abusive marriage with Danny's grandfather at the time of his mother's disappearance, but the old man is dead now, so they are thinking of placing Danny with her."

"Will it be soon?" Beth asked.

"It's still touch and go, but I've got faith that he will recover." His face grew still. "I feel some connection to that boy. And I suppose it's right for him to be reunited with what is left of his family." A look of sadness passed quickly across his face and Beth was reminded of his own lonely upbringing. "But I wish I could take him home with me. I would protect him." His chin was stuck out defiantly.

Beth remembered the young man who used to protect her from her own daredevil doings on Stutter Creek.

"I want to see him," she said. "I want to see Allie, too. And Turk, my savior! When I heard him crashing through the brush, well, I knew I was going to be okay." She ducked her head a bit because she didn't trust herself to look John in the eye. She wasn't sure what she might see there. Or what he might see in hers.

Laying his big hand over her smaller ones, he said: "Turk is not the only one who was crashing through that forest," he said. "It would have killed me if we hadn't arrived in time. I barely found you again . . ." He left the rest of the sentence bare, but Beth could fill in the blank. She felt the same way.

"Thank you," she said looking her friend in the eye at last. "Thank you both." Then she smiled and clasped his hand to her chest.

Weeks later they talked about how the man who had tried to kill her had died. John admitted that he might have known that the handcuff chain was cutting off his airway. "But I'm not exactly sure," he said. "It was pretty intense tumbling down that mountain locked in a death roll with a madman." He looked deeply into Beth's eyes when he told her that. "Does that scare you?"

Beth thought for a moment. "No," she admitted. "Maybe it should, hearing that you may have killed him knowingly . . . but I can tell you this," she squared her shoulders. "I would have done it myself if I could."

John's shock showed on his face.

Beth held her breath. She wasn't going to lie. She hated the man they now knew as Kurt Graham. He was a monster. He'd killed two women, perhaps three if his wife was his first victim as everyone suspected, and he'd tried to kill both her and Allie. But the thing that bothered her more than any other was the fact that he had used his own son to do it. She knew he would have killed Danny eventually. Or let him die, which was the same thing in her book.

After a moment, John pulled her onto his lap. They were sitting in his renovated cabin, watching the sunset through the picture window. "You have every right to say that," he admitted. "And the fact that you're brave enough to admit it, well, that's one reason I never settled for any other woman."

"I can't wait until we hear if our foster parent application has been approved," she said.

John smiled and stroked his beard, deep in thought. "Do you really think there's a chance we will get to bring Danny home?"

Beth nodded. "I feel like it was meant to be," she said. "Something good has to come out of this tragedy. And the caseworker told me just yesterday that the grandmother wants to meet us. She's quite elderly, and she's decided she might not be up to the task of caring for Danny for the next fifteen to twenty years. She actually seems to want what's best for Danny."

He reached over and took her hand; twisting the simple gold band he'd placed there a week earlier. "How will I ever explain to him that I'm the one who killed his father? Won't that set us up for failure as a family?"

Beth shrugged. "You saved his life. He will understand that. I'm not saying it will be easy, but I know we have what it takes to give that boy the home he deserves. And once we're approved as foster parents, and the grandmother gives her consent, then we can start adoption proceedings." She took his face between her palms. "But I hope that isn't the only reason you married me so quickly."

John threw his head back and laughed. "Actually, I was going to tell you later . . . but the real reason is because . . . I'm pregnant."

Then he kissed her, and she grinned, kissing him right back.

Turk whuffed softly and stuck his big head under her elbow.

"Yes," she said, "I love you too."

Meet the Author

Ann Swann is the author of **All For Love**, a contemporary love story also published by 5 Prince Publishing. She is also the author of **Stevie-girl and the Phantom Pilot, and Stevie-girl and the Phantom Student,** tales of the supernatural. Ann has also written numerous award winning short stories. She lives in West Texas with her husband and several rescue pets. She loves libraries and book stores and owns two different e-readers just for fun. Her to-be-read list has taken on a life of its own. She calls it Herman.

www.ingramcontent.com/pod-product-compliance
Lightning Source LLC
Chambersburg PA
CBHW030324020726
47493CB00004B/1152